Snowed In
WITH THE
WOLF

HAWKE

You know what? *Fuck* elves. Seriously.

I clicked off the television and chucked the remote across the couch, cursing myself for getting sucked into that sappy holiday movie bullshit... *again*. Another two hours of my life I'd never get back, and to top it off, now my beer was warm.

I tipped the bottle back anyway, pouring half of it down my throat, the rest dripping down my chin and onto my bare chest. It hardly registered. I was numb from the inside out, and the six-pack I'd already polished off had done nothing to improve my mood.

That's what I got for grabbing the "Holiday Harvest" brew by mistake. Holiday Harvest my ass—more like Merry Marketing Scam. Suck out half the alcohol, sprinkle in some pumpkin spice, and jack up the price for all the suckers willing to pay double for anything with a cartoon reindeer stamped on the package.

Add it to the long list of things I fucking *hated* about this time of year.

Far as I was concerned, Christmas was played out. It wasn't always like that—as a kid, I'd loved waking up with my little sister, racing her down the stairs to find our mom cooking up a big-ass breakfast, our meager tree lit up like Rockefeller Center. Never knew our dad, and we didn't have much in the way of luxury items, but I never felt like I was missing out back then. Mom had always made damn sure of that.

But seventeen years ago, my mother and sister died in a wreck, and with nowhere else to turn, I threw myself into the darkest, most shadowy corners of the U.S. military, volunteering for missions so dangerous, so horrendous, the CIA told everyone else they didn't exist. *I* didn't exist.

I was a good soldier. A good mercenary, if you want to real truth of it. Did my job, kept my mouth shut, collected the cash. But then? They fucking turned on me.

And in a matter of weeks, I went from a good soldier to a fucking lab rat, every forced injection another notch on some corporate stiff's belt, all part of some big bullshit dream to engineer the perfect fighter.

Yeah, right. Should've done a little more fine-tuning on that formula, because what they got instead was a fucking mutant wolf. A lab-created shifter with no pack, no family, and—by the time they were done with me—no heart.

At some point without my permission, while I'd faced off with assassins half my age and drank my own piss in the desert just to stay alive, while I'd suffered through those first few uncontrollable shifts from man into raging beast with an unquenchable lust for violence and bloodshed, most of my happy holiday memories turned into ghosts.

And now, even though I had the wolf under control and my military career was six months in the rearview, I still hated this time of year.

Christmas? Nothing more than an industry designed to make you feel like you didn't have enough—presents, money, food, friends, family, love. All of it.

It pissed me off.

Of course, if Santa ever stuffed his ample ass down my chimney again, I wouldn't think twice about making a few requests. The first? Give me a soft, warm place to bury my dick—preferably a woman who knew how to be handled. A feisty redhead with just a pinch of nice wrapped up inside a naughty-as-hell package.

Perfection.

I'd take my time with a woman like that, running my tongue along every curve of her flesh, savoring the taste. Or maybe I'd tease her first, making her beg for release as I fisted her hair and slammed into her from behind, my balls smacking against that round, ripe ass as she arched her back and screamed my name...

I closed my eyes, teeth grazing my lower lip.

Fuck, yeah. Just like that...

It was a familiar fantasy—redheads were my *absolute* kryptonite—and my cock was already standing at attention. I unbuttoned my jeans and shoved a hand inside, gripping myself hard, wondering if I should drag my imaginary girlfriend into the shower to take care of business. But after a minute of serving up the usual play-by-play, my imagination stalled out. The redhead faded from my mind, and when I opened my eyes, reality came crashing back into my lap.

Nothing had changed, and nothing ever would. I was a fucking cartoon nightmare, a used-up science experiment sitting around with my dick in one hand and a bottle of booze in the other, hiding out from a world that'd chewed my ass up and spit me out hard.

I was utterly alone. Alone in my head. Alone in my pain. Alone in my beautiful but secluded cabin on the outskirts of Rocky Mountain National Park, eight thousand feet above sea level and a million miles away from anything that'd ever mattered to me.

And that's how I'd die.

"Go fuck yourself, Santa. I hope you and your reindeer get buried in a fucking avalanche. And you can take the entire months of November, December, and January with you, because I'm done."

Not bothering to zip up my pants, I got up from the couch and dragged my ass into the kitchen, rooting around for the bottle I'd been saving for more than a decade.

It had no label, and the glass was so dark and dusty it looked like an antique. I pried off the homemade wax seal with my pocket knife and yanked out the cork, letting the stuff take its first breath of American air.

I'd received it as a Christmas gift during my first mission in El Salvador from a wiry, coked-out arms dealer named Kiko, and for some shit-ass reason that escaped me now, I'd promised myself I wouldn't open it until—and unless—I survived. The mission, the month, the year, the mission after that, the orders, the threats, the bribes, the experiments, the transition, the hunger... Every fucking minute until all that shit was behind me and I finally had a place to call home.

I'd carried that bottle around all this time, smuggling it from one shithole of the world to another, in and out of every kind of nightmare imaginable until it finally ended up here in Colorado.

The end of the line.

I was six months retired now, thirty-four fucking years old, had more dirty money than I'd be able to spend in a dozen lifetimes, and most days I still wasn't sure I'd survived.

Hell, most days I still wasn't sure I even *wanted* to.

But tonight, for right now, I was still breathing.

Had to count for something.

I poured myself a double and raised the glass in front of me, eyeing the amber liquid in the light. Looked and smelled like good shit, despite its age and questionable origins.

"*Feliz Navidad*, Kiko. Wherever the fuck *you* are."

The whiskey burned all the way down, lighting a fire in my belly that quickly spread to my limbs. I poured another shot, grabbed the glass and the bottle, and reclaimed my well-worn seat on the couch.

The snow was piling up like a bitch outside, banking against the first-floor windows and wrapping the evergreens in thick, white blankets. Normally, my wolf loved running in the snow, but this shit was too brutal, even for me. Had to be about twenty below out there, and the howl of the wind was so lonely it made my chest ache.

But fuck it, right? I was warm inside, the timber-framed log home blocking out all the cold, fire roaring in the stone hearth beside me, fridge and pantry stocked from a recent supply run, no one around for miles.

What did I have to bitch about, really?

Considering that the pinnacle of last year's yuletide festivities had involved storming a tulip warehouse in Holland and gunning down a bunch of ecstasy dealers at the behest of the CIA, this year's Christmas Eve was already a stellar improvement, Holiday Harvest aside.

It was my first Christmas alone, and that's just how I liked it now. No dick-measuring, black ops mercenaries. No hiding my wolf when all I wanted to do was shift and hunt, to satiate this wild hunger without some military scientist sticking needles up my ass. No gunfire. No creeping through the shadows in seventy-five pounds of tactical gear, trying to decipher who was the good guy, who was the monster, what the fuck side I was supposed to be on. Just me and my girl, Bella, the only living soul I still gave a fuck about.

"Bella! Come here, baby."

The eighty-pound, black-and-tan German Shepherd tumbled down the stairs, tail wagging, tongue flapping as she leapt up next to me on the couch and shoved her snout straight into my armpit.

I set my whiskey on the end table and scratched

behind her ears, nuzzling her face. "What kind of trouble are you getting into up there, huh?"

She whimpered, then sighed, dropping her head onto my thigh.

Translation: guilty as fuck.

"Yeah, that's what I thought," I said. "Stay out of my closet."

She'd already chewed through my favorite hiking boots, half dozen pairs of socks, and an old, unopened box of condoms left by cabin's previous owner which had resulted in a trip to the vet and a procedure the dog would likely never forget.

But no matter how much trouble she caused, I still loved her crazy ass. I'd found her soon after I bought this place last summer, tortured and emaciated, left for dead in the woods out back. She'd been *this* close to becoming dinner for a mountain lion, but my wolf chased the beast off. I shifted back and carried her to my truck, got her checked out in town. She had no tags, no license, no chip, which was probably a good thing. If I ever found the motherfuckers who'd done that to her, I'd make damn sure the neighborhood mountain lions had *plenty* to eat then.

People were real assholes. Best to stay the fuck away from them.

If only I could get away from myself.

I blew out a dark sigh. Until I figured out *that* little fucking secret to a happy life, I'd have to settle for the next best thing: drinking myself into a stupor, jerking off, and passing out, in no particular order.

I clicked the television back on and scrolled through the satellite channels. A few more sips of that whiskey, and even the Hallmark channel was starting to look good again. They were showing another bullshit it's-a-God-damn-Christmas-miracle,   ain't-our-family-swell kind of movies, but the chick playing the mom was hot as hell.

"Hello, MILF," I said, turning up the volume and kicking back on the sofa. I let out a huge belch, and Bella jerked up her head and barked at me, taking off upstairs again.

Eh, no accounting for taste.

I didn't know what the fuck was in Kiko's magic booze, but by the third pour, my entire body was buzzing and relaxed, my head swimming pleasantly as the movie droned on. The mom was getting hotter by the minute— possibly an effect of the booze, but by then, I was all outta fucks to give.

Feeling primed up again, I slid my hand down the front of my pants and palmed my cock. This time, the bastard jumped to life in an instant, hot, stiff, and ready to rock.

That's fucking more like it, asshole.

I muted the TV, closed my eyes, and leaned my head back, calling up another image of my fantasy girl, flat on her back for some sixty-nine action, my tongue spearing her pussy as I fucked that hot, wet mouth.

My cock was smooth as silk and hard as ice, and with every stroke, I imagined her lush, pink mouth taking me deeper. She wanted it bad, her legs trembling as I claimed that sweet pussy with my mouth. And this girl... *fuck*, she was naughty. She couldn't get enough of me, bucking against my face, her thighs wet and glistening as she begged me to eat her harder and faster...

My balls tightened, the pressure building at the base. I was getting close, and I didn't give a fuck what kind of mess I was in for. I needed this release, was fucking desperate for it. *Yes.* I rocked my hips, bearing down hard as I stroked my aching cock, picturing those glossy pink lips sucking me, taking me in deeper... deeper... deeper...

Fuck, yeah. Right there. Right fucking—
CRASH!

Something clattered to the floor in the bedroom, and the damn dog shot back down the stairs like a bat out of hell, yanking me right out of my fantasy at the worst fucking time.

Strikeout.

"Damn it, Bella." I whipped my head around to see what the big deal was. She was in the kitchen, yelping and barking, her tail wagging as she furiously pawed the windows in the breakfast nook.

Someone had to be out there.

Fuck.

I rose from the couch, grabbing my hoodie and shoving my arms through.

I joined Bella in the kitchen and peered out the windows, but I couldn't see shit through the blowing snow, so I clicked on the closed-circuit TV mounted under the cabinets and checked the security cameras. The screen was a frosty white blur, but one image came through crystal clear.

A car.

Jammed into a snowbank at the end of my driveway.

Sideways.

2

MADDIE

T was the night before Christmas, and no matter how hard I freaking tried, things were just *not* going according to plan.

I kicked open my car door, slamming it hard against the snowbank I'd just plowed into. The rental car was definitely dead, and I was pretty sure I'd hit something —a fairly large boulder type-of-something—on the downward slide that'd landed me here.

Shit, shit, *shit* topped with sprinkles.

My heart dropped into my stomach. There was no way I'd make it to Christmas dinner now.

Still... It could've been worse.

I was alive, right? Stranded with no vehicle and no cell service in the middle of Nowheresville, Colorado during a raging blizzard, but alive.

"Go me, beating the odds once again!"

Reaching inside my scarf, I fished out the locket I wore around my neck and gave it a grateful kiss. It was a familiar ritual; I'd flatlined and come back enough times that they'd written me up in medical journals, and doctors were still making vague predictions about my expiration date, just as they'd been doing every year since I was born.

But just like *I'd* been doing for those last twenty-five years, I kept right on proving them wrong.

Then again, the night was young, and I wasn't out of the woods yet. Literally. I glanced around, taking in the sight. Deep, dark forests of snow-covered ponderosa pines as far as the eye could see.

People died in the woods all the time, especially in the winter. Swallowed up by an avalanche and never heard from again.

I shook my head, clearing my thoughts before they turned any more morbid.

Time for a little tough love.

"Maddie Lockwood? Get your cute little Christmas ass out of the car, assess the situation, and make a plan."

There was just enough room to wedge myself through the opening without ruining my elf costume, and when I was finally free of the two-ton death trap, I nearly cried with relief. As it turned out, I wasn't in a ditch at the bottom of a forested ravine as I'd feared, but in a driveway. At the very top of the rise was a cozy-looking, two-story log cabin nestled in the trees, smoke rising from the chimney, the whole place lit up inside.

A postcard-perfect shot, and it looked like someone was home.

"Thank you, Father Christmas!"

All I had to do was make my way up there, knock on the door, and turn on the charm. With a bit of Christmas luck and the magic of the elves, maybe they'd offer me a nice, steaming mug of hot cocoa and some fresh-baked cookies while I waited for the tow truck, and I'd be delivered to my parents' vacation rental in time to surprise them before Dad gobbled up the last of the pecan-dusted sweet potatoes.

Leaving everything else behind, I hauled myself over the hood, then dropped down onto the driveway on the other side into powdery, knee-deep snow. I wasn't wearing much—I'd changed into my outfit at the rental car place at Denver International, planning to arrive dressed as Santa's little helper, all part of the big surprise. But now the bitter wind tore into my flesh, giving me *another* sort of surprise. And if you've never gotten frostbite of the hoo-ha, well... allow me to save you the trouble.

Zero stars, do not recommend.

The wind kicked up, the icy air making my lungs burn, and I was pretty sure my toes were turning blue as I stomped a path up the unplowed driveway in my cute little elf shoes. But it would be worth it. Hot chocolate, a toasty fire... Maybe they'd even want to sing a few carols! I had all the classics memorized.

When I finally reached the front porch, I could barely breathe. At least the porch was partially enclosed, blocking out the worst of the wind—a temporary reprieve.

I raised my fist, but before I could pound on the door, it swung inward, revealing...

A mirage.

It *had* to be a mirage. A snow mirage. Was that a thing? Or were mirages limited to the desert? Either way, there was no other explanation for the vision standing before me.

The guy was in his early thirties, with wavy black hair that stuck up everywhere, and a strong, defined jaw covered in the perfect amount of I-don't-give-a-damn scruff. He'd opened the door in his bare feet, wearing nothing but a pair of low-slung jeans all undone, a thin hoodie, and a scowl that sent the kind of shivers down my spine that had nothing to do with the cold. Just like his pants, the hoodie was unzipped, revealing a *serious* set of abs.

His muscular chest was slick with a light sheen of sweat.

I must've interrupted his workout...

Forget the damn cookies. Good lord, I wanted to lick *him*. Drop to my knees, press my face against his stomach, and run my tongue all over that perfectly sculpted body...

Oh, god. What the hell is wrong *with me?*

I'd just survived a near death experience, I was missing the epic Lockwood family Christmas celebration, and I was freezing my little snow globes off—yet *that's* where my brain went? To licking a total stranger's sweaty abs? Honestly!

Note to self: next time, ask the docs to examine my head instead of my heart.

"What can I do for you?" the sexy stranger asked, finally meeting my eyes. But once he pinned me with his steely gaze, all I could do was keep on gaping. His body was a thing of beauty, but those eyes were downright hypnotic, the color of flint and just as hard. The kind of eyes that hid a thousand secrets. The kind that broke a thousand hearts.

For a moment, the mysterious stranger and I just stood there, not speaking, locked in the most intense stare. Obvious hotness aside, there was something so familiar about him, so... *magnetic.* When I opened my mouth to respond, the first words that popped into my head were—inexplicably—*I missed you.*

He pulled the door shut behind him and stepped out onto the porch, and the moment between us passed.

A cough wheezed its way out of my chest.

"Merry... Merry Christmas," I finally managed, my hand pressed to my heart. Poor thing was banging like a trapped animal, and I needed to slow it down with some deep breathing, but the icy air was still gnawing away at my lungs.

"You okay?" he asked, those flint eyes narrowing. "You're not looking too hot."

"Can I... can I..." I swallowed hard. A wave of dizziness slammed into my body, throwing me off balance. I closed my eyes to stop the spinning, but it was too late. The porch tipped sideways, my legs buckled beneath me, and then I was pitching forward with all the grace of kid learning to ice skate, crashing headlong into those sexy abs.

The man had amazing instincts. He darted forward and grabbed me, steadying me against his bare chest and saving me from hitting the ground.

I was safe and secure in his strong, muscular arms, but my head felt like a balloon on a string, my thoughts floating away on the breeze.

"You're really warm," I said suddenly, giggling like an

idiot. I was breathing hard, the lack of oxygen in my blood making me goofy. "Like, *super* warm."

I grinned up at him.

He scowled down at me.

And then my world went black.

3

HAWKE

There's an elf on my shelf.

I blinked. Twice.

Fuck *me*. I hadn't even hit the bottle all that hard yet, and now I was straight-up seeing things.

"Hey," I said, looking down at the elf in my arms. Her eyes fluttered closed, her body slack. Breath escaped her mouth in frantic white puffs, and even through her costume, I could feel the heartbeat machine-gunning in her chest.

No way. No fucking way. The last thing I needed was Santa's little helper dying in my arms in the middle of a damn blizzard.

I gave her a firm but gentle shake.

"Come on, now. Don't do this to me." I pressed the

back of my hand to her cheek—she felt like a popsicle. "Wake up, baby. Wake up."

Her eyes opened again, then widened, a fresh blush competing with the frigid air to make her cheeks pink. She disentangled herself from my hold and stood up on her own two feet again, but I kept a grip on her arms, just in case.

"You with me now?" I asked.

She was gaping at me with huge, blue eyes that stood out like sapphires in the snow, those cheeks turning pinker by the minute. Locks of flame-red hair spilled out from beneath a sparkly white hat, stark against her green scarf. And the rest of that scandalous outfit? God *damn.* A tight red ballerina dress that barely skimmed the tops of her thighs, red-and-white striped stockings, and one of those useless little half-sweaters girls wore that did absolutely nothing to hide the diamond-hard nipples poking out beneath.

She looked like a candy-cane cupcake, just begging for me to sink my teeth right in.

My cock stirred at the thought.

Hey, remember me, asshole?

I released her and took a step back, zipping up my pants and adjusting myself before things got uncomfortable. That one-track mind of mine was going to get me into *serious* trouble one of these days.

"Thank... thank you." The girl was panting again, a mittened hand pressed to her chest as she struggled to catch her breath.

"You okay?" I asked.

"Fine. Just... it's probably the altitude. And the stomping-through-the-snow part. Your driveway isn't exactly plowed."

"Wasn't expecting company."

"But it's Christmas Eve," she said, as though that explained shit. After a beat, she narrowed her eyes, her nose wrinkling in the cutest fucking way imaginable. "Sir. Are you *drunk*?"

"Not drunk enough," I muttered, which was damn lucky for her. Any more inebriated, and I would've had zero judgment, zero inhibition, *zero* reservations about dragging her little elf ass inside, pinning her against the wall, and finding out *exactly* what she was hiding underneath those candy-cane stockings.

"*Oooh*-kay then." Her breathing seemed to normalize, thank fuck—one less thing for me to deal with. "Sorry to bother you at an obviously bad time, but I kind of crashed my car into your driveway, and now it won't start, and my phone has no service out here, and I *really* need to get to my parents' cabin before dinner's over or it'll turn into this whole *thing*, because my mom is super high maintenance and I didn't even tell them I was coming, and I always mess up Christmas every single year, but this year I planned out this whole surprise for them, so I was hoping I could—"

"Slow down, Cupcake." Whether it was the booze or that hot little outfit, my ability to concentrate was seriously compromised. I could barely follow her mile-a-minute ramble. "What do you mean, you 'kind of' crashed your car?"

She lowered her eyes and shrugged, nibbling on her lower lip, and fuck, the sight of her teeth against that plump, rosy flesh made my cock twitch all over again. All I could think about was how that lip would feel between my teeth, what kind of sounds she'd make if I bit down on it and sucked...

"I lost the road," she went on. "Or it lost me. I don't know. It's whiteout conditions, right? I'm driving along, trying to figure out where I took a wrong turn, and all of a sudden I can't steer. Can't stop. I'm just spinning and sliding down this hill, no control, just hoping and praying that when it's all over, I land somewhere soft." She smiled innocently, finally meeting my eyes again, her eyes full of a sweet hope I hadn't seen in years. Decades. "And ta-da! Here I am!"

I grunted out a laugh. "Hate to break it to you, Cupcake, but I ain't exactly somewhere soft."

She looked away again, another blush creeping up her neck.

Damn, that looks good on her. Wonder what else makes her blush...

"Could I maybe just... use your phone?" she asked.

I leaned back against the door, crossing my arms over my chest. Flustered was a good look on her, and I liked being the one who'd put it there. "Nope."

That got her attention.

She stared me down, hands on her hips, red hair licking her shoulders like fire. She was the textbook definition of "adorable when you're mad," but I wisely kept that little observation to myself. The last time I'd thrown that phrase at a redhead, I damn near lost a testicle. Had to flee Spain on a Greek merchant ship in the middle of the night just to avoid the fallout.

"What are you smirking at?" she demanded.

"Nothing, Cupcake. Not a damn thing."

"Dude." She yanked off her hat and scratched her head. Her hair was wild with static electricity, her eyes blazing. "Seriously? *Seriously.* It's deadly cold out here. I'm freezing my ass off in this elf costume. My car crash-landed at the end of your driveway. I literally fainted in your arms. It's Christmas Eve. Could you maybe just be, I don't know, a *little* less of a prick?"

"Can't." I shrugged, stifling a laugh. Live entertainment was hard to come by around these parts—I'd take my amusement where I could get it. "Phone line's been out for hours. Internet's down, and my cell works for shit up here even on a sunny day. Satellite TV's still holding on, though, if you're up for a movie."

I turned the doorknob, and the instant I cracked open the door, Bella yelped and darted out past me. She nearly tackled the girl, sniffing her up and down, sticking her snout into places that made me curse the day I was born a man instead of a dog.

"Oh my god!" the girl squealed, her annoyance melting away in an instant. "Who is *this* beautiful baby?" She dropped to her knees and scratched behind Bella's ears with both hands, laughing wildly as Bella licked her face. "Hi, pretty girl! Aren't you just the sweetest thing ever? What's your name?"

"Her name's *Traitor*," I grumbled, reaching out to grab the hunk of fur at the back of Bella's neck. "Also known as Sleeping Outside Tonight."

"Aww," the girl said, still talking to Bella. She stuck out her bottom lip in an exaggerated pout. "Somebody's got a grumpy daddy. Huh, puppy?"

"I ain't grumpy, and she ain't a puppy. Get inside, Bella." The dog nudged my hand, giving it a good licking. She knew I'd never make her sleep outside—she had me wrapped around her little paw, and she played that for all it was worth.

Typical woman.

I finally wedged her back into the cabin, pulling the door against my legs so she couldn't escape again.

"She really is beautiful." The girl stood up and turned those big blue eyes back on me. "I had a German Shepherd when I was a kid. I called him Turkey."

"You named your dog Turkey?"

"He was born on Thanksgiving. But we had to give him away because I was allergic. But don't worry, I'm not anymore. Allergic, I mean. Not to animals. Only avocados, red dye number forty, mangos, certain kinds of seeds, and—"

"Stop," I said. "Please stop talking." Holy *fuck*. How the hell could a girl who'd crashed her car into a driveway looking like she'd just wandered off the set of Santa's Naughty Little Helpers talk so damn much? I'd only known her for five minutes, and I was already exhausted. "You coming inside, or are you just gonna chill out here?"

She fucking cracked *up*. No warning, no pause, girl just busted out laughing like it was amateur night at the Improv and I was the star of the show.

A tiny sliver of ice broke off from the solid block around my heart.

No woman, anywhere, ever, in any language, had ever appreciated my corny puns.

God damn, I might have to keep this one...

"Thanks," she said. "I needed that." She blotted her watery eyes with the end of her scarf, then let out a not-so-happy sigh. "But I *really* need to get to my family. Maybe you can help me push the car out of the snowbank? See if it starts up again?"

Not fucking likely.

"Whatever you say, Cupcake. Just give me a sec." I reached inside the door for my coat and work boots and geared up. Didn't need them, really—the wolf inside me made the man a lot stronger than a regular human. But the woman might start asking questions if I trudged out into the snow in my bare feet. "Be right back, Bella. Behave yourself."

"Oh, also?" the girl said as I pulled the door closed. "I'm ninety-nine percent sure I hit something on the way into your driveway, because there was a big thud, and after that, the car started making this weird grinding noise, like... grrrr-*chunk*, grrrr-*chunk*, grrrr—"

"Chunk." I held up a hand. "Got it."

"You know, maybe it's better if you just give me a ride." She bounced on her toes, her eyes doing some kind of cute puppy-dog thing that was hard as hell to resist. "Their cabin is just on the other side of Route Seven, on Spruce?"

"Route Seven?" I shook my head. "That's twenty miles from here."

"It's not *that* far."

"You see anyone out there right now? You pass a single car on these roads on your way up?"

"No."

"And why do you suppose that is?"

"I know it's icy," she said, still bouncing. "But you probably drive a crazy souped-up Hummer or something, right? Please?"

Those eyes had some kind of mojo that in any other circumstance might've had me on my knees by now, preferably with my tongue buried deep inside her, but I held firm.

"Negative. For one thing, your car is blocking my exit. For another, you *do* realize what's happening out there, right?" I jerked my head toward the expanse beyond my porch, a sea of white in all directions. You couldn't even tell where the sky ended and the snow-drifts began. "Only an idiot would drive in this shit."

The bouncing stopped. Her eyes glazed with tears, and suddenly I felt like the biggest asshole walking.

"An idiot," she said, her lip quivering. *Aww, hell. Here we go. Three, two, one, and...* "Or maybe just a person who loves her family and hasn't been able to spend Christmas with them in forever, and is looking forward more than anything in the world to holding her two-month-old nephew for the very first time, and surprising her twin four-year-old nieces with a visit from Santa's helper, and giving her parents home-made Christmas presents she spent *months* working on. But it's cool, I get it. You're busy. You don't do visitors. You're the Grinch. I'm an idiot. Glad we cleared that up. So thanks for your time, Mr. I Hate Christmas, but I think I'll take my chances with a *different* crazy mountain recluse."

She wiped her eyes with the scarf again and turned on her heel, stomping down the porch stairs and back out into the frigid snow, red hair blowing out behind her.

I sighed. I didn't know jack about this girl, but somehow I knew—way down deep in the icy wasteland of my heart—I was done for. Absolutely, positively done for.

Fucking gingers, man.

I hopped off the porch and caught up with her in two strides, grabbing her arms in a tight grip.

"A *different* crazy mountain recluse? Yeah, I don't think so, Cupcake."

4

MADDIE

Douche bag. He was definitely a douche bag. But not a psychopath—an important distinction. I could always tell about people. And anyway, he was kind of right. Stranded in the middle of nowhere, ice and snow blanketing the high country, I had little in the way of an escape route.

Didn't mean I had to make it easy on him, though. Not after the rude way he'd treated me.

I jerked away from his grip. "What do you want?"

The guy shrugged out of his wool-lined flannel coat and held it out for me, but I didn't budge.

"Humor me," he said, tossing it at me as he stomped past.

"Whatever." Secretly grateful, I slipped my arms into the huge sleeves and zipped up. He'd only worn it for a few minutes, but the heat lingered, wrapping me in a full-bodied hug.

And holy *hell*, the scent of him. So. Freaking. Amazing. It was like evergreens and cinnamon and soap and the great outdoors and just... *him.* Male. Hot. Filling my senses and making my insides swirl.

I wonder what he smells like up close, like right around that sexy spot where his jaw meets his ear...

"You got a name, Cupcake?" the guy called out. He was already halfway down the driveway and hadn't even turned around to see if I was following.

What a jerk!

A super sexy, good-smelling jerk!

"Madison Lockwood," I said, scrambling to catch up. At least this time I could follow in his footsteps and avoid some of the snow. "Most people call me Maddie. Except my mom, who insists on calling me Mash, which she's done since I was three and couldn't pronounce my own name. Um... where are we going?"

"To see what we can do about your piece of shit car blocking the end of my driveway."

"It's not mine. It's a rental. And why do you care about the driveway? I thought you weren't expecting company?"

He turned to shoot me a glare over his shoulder.

"Right," I mumbled. "Allergic to sarcasm. Got it."

At the end of the driveway, the snowdrifts had gotten so high they now made a cozy alcove that blocked the wind. The blizzard was harsh, but the snow was beautiful—big, soft flakes piling up everywhere.

"We should totally make a snowman," I said, handing over the car keys. "This is the perfect snow for it."

"Knock yourself out." He grabbed my sleeve and tugged me out of the way, kicking chunks of ice and snow off the car. Once he had enough room, he wedged open the driver's side door and crammed himself into the seat, banging his knees on the steering wheel in the process.

"You might want to adjust the—"

"Got it." Cursing under his breath, he shoved the seat back and looked around the interior, surprised. "I didn't know they rented manual transmission cars anymore."

"I had to book it special," I said. "And they gouged me on the price. But it's the only way I'll drive these mountain roads, even in the summer. I like the control."

He held my gaze a moment, and I could've sworn I saw the hint of a smile twitching at the corners of his mouth, but then it was gone, straight back to business.

The business of getting me out of here.

"Well, let's see what she's got." He jammed the key

into the ignition, stepped on the brake and the clutch, and gave the engine a crank.

The car sounded like it was dying a slow death.

"That's the grrr-chunky noise I told you about," I added helpfully.

"So I gathered." He tried to start it again in second gear, but the clutch just wouldn't catch, and that noise was getting worse every time. He turned it off and shook his head.

"So what's your name, tough guy?" I asked, stepping back again as he climbed out. "Wait, don't tell me. Blade. No, Gunner. You definitely look like a Gunner."

"I hospitalized a guy named Gunner in a fight once. That count?" He handed me the keys, then dropped onto his hands and knees and stuck his head under the car to investigate, slowly making his way around the whole thing.

A fight? *Damn.* The thought of him getting violent should *not* have turned me on so much. Clearly, the altitude was messing with my head.

"No, it doesn't count," I said. "So you're not a Gunner or a Blade. Rock? Mack? Jack? Yes, Jack fits you. Rugged, classic—"

"Hawke Stevens." He climbed out from under the car and stood to face me again, dusting the snow from his hands.

I waited, but he didn't offer any additional details. "Not much for regular-type conversation, are you, Hawke Stevens?"

"You converse enough for the both of us."

I pressed my lips together, ignoring the burn in my cheeks.

"Here's the situation," Hawke said. "Bent axle, two bent rims, and that tranny's FUBAR—and that's just the shit I could see. You ain't going anywhere tonight, Cupcake. Not in that heap."

I knew it was stupid to hope, but still. Hearing him say it out loud like that made it official: Maddie Lockwood, miracle of miracles, had ruined Christmas once again.

The disappointment must've shown all over my face, because suddenly Hawke was looking at me with... well, it wasn't sympathy exactly, but close enough.

"Thanks anyway for trying," I said. "Sorry to waste your time."

"Don't sweat it." Hawke put a hand on my shoulder, his calloused fingers unintentionally grazing my neck beneath the scarf. After all his gruffness, the touch felt strangely intimate, sending shock waves of warmth rippling through my body.

"But as much as I *love* shooting the shit out here in the middle of a storm," he continued, "I got a blazing fire and a bottle of illegal whiskey I'd like to get back to, preferably before my balls freeze off."

"I... oh. Of course." I smiled and stepped back from his touch, cheeks burning again, despite the cold.

Time for plan B. I might not be able to get the car moving again, but maybe I could use the onboard nav system to signal a tow truck or... something. Not that tow trucks were running right now, given the treacherous conditions.

Shoot.

I unzipped his jacket and slid it off my shoulders, my entire body grieving the loss of the warmth and his intoxicating, masculine scent. "Thanks again for your help, Hawke. Um... okay, then. I guess I'll just... right. Merry Christmas, then."

I shoved the jacket toward him, but Hawke gave me a crooked, wicked grin that sent a bolt of desire straight to my core.

"Nice try, Cupcake." He closed the distance between us and jerked the coat out of my hands, wrapping me up in it again like I was his own personal Christmas gift. With a firm grip on the collar, he pulled me so close I could see the snowflakes melting on his feathery black eyelashes, feel the hot steam of his breath as it puffed white against my cheeks.

In a growl that made my panties wet, he said, "I told

you, you ain't going anywhere tonight. Except inside. With me."

The grumpy barbarian held my gaze, those flint-gray eyes boring into mine as if he'd issued an order rather than an offer.

Holy hell.

I'd been planning this trip for months, so determined and excited to surprise my family, to finally enjoy Christmas outside of a hospital bed. I was so, so close, too—I'd made it all the way from my apartment in New York City, from buses and planes and shuttles to the rental car, across highways and through tunnels and up the side of a damn mountain, only to crash a mere twenty miles from my destination.

Despite all that, the strange, magnetic pull of Hawke Stevens was too strong to resist—even if he *was* a little rough around the edges.

He finally released his grip on the collar, and I pressed a hand to my chest, feeling the familiar tiny lump of the locket, warm and comforting against my skin. Behind it, my heart beat strong and steady once more, calming my nerves.

Seeing no other sane options for the moment—at least until the storm let up—I sighed and hit the button on the key fob, popping the trunk. "I need my things."

Hawke looked inside. "There's enough luggage in there for an entire platoon. You need all of it?"

"Just the big one. The rest can stay."

Hawke hauled out my suitcase, hefting it over his shoulder and slamming the trunk shut. "Let's go."

Without a backward glance, he walked back up to the cabin, stomping a fresh path for me through the snow.

I took a deep breath, blew it out in a white plume, and followed him, a new warmth spreading inside me.

Yeah. Maybe a little "rough around the edges" was just what I needed tonight.

Not like things could get any worse, right?

5

HAWKE

W hat's your poison?"

I took a clean mug out of the cupboard, eyeing up my guest seated at the kitchen table. Bella curled up on the floor at her feet as if Maddie were already a regular fixture.

Other than the realtor who'd sold me the cabin this summer and a lost hunter who'd needed directions, I'd never invited another person inside the doorway, let alone to sit at the table where I ate my meals.

It was surreal.

Maddie was still snuggled inside my jacket, her legs tucked up underneath her on the chair, watching me with those intense blue eyes. Now that her face had returned to its normal color, a faint spray of freckles stood out across her nose and cheeks.

Fucking adorable.

She considered my offer for a full minute, then finally said, "I think I'll have hot cocoa."

Damn.

"No can do."

Her nose wrinkled. "It's Christmas Eve and you don't have any hot chocolate?"

"Maybe you haven't noticed, but this ain't exactly Santa's workshop." I slammed the mug on the table, harder than I'd meant to.

Why hadn't I thought to pick up hot chocolate on my supply run the other day?

Because you weren't expecting a hot, demanding-as-fuck, cocoa-drinking redhead to come crashing into your driveway, dumbass.

"I got coffee," I said. "Leaded and unleaded. I got whiskey, which I ain't keen on sharing. I got shitty Christmas beer. I got heavy cream. And I got water. Pick one. Hell, pick two—I'm in a generous mood."

"You have Christmas beer, but no Christmas tree?"

I clamped my jaw shut before I said something *really* rude.

"Okay, okay. Coffee," she said, undeterred. "Leaded, with cream. But don't make it *too* strong. Caffeine makes me kind of spazzy."

"So, decaf then."

"Hawke!"

I shot her a glare, then got to work. I didn't have a coffeemaker, just did it pour-over style with an old bandanna for a filter. She watched me with great interest as I attached the bandanna to the mug with a rubber band and dumped some ground coffee on top—a little regular, followed by a whole heap of decaf, hoping she wouldn't notice the ol' switcheroo.

"Does this mean you don't have any Christmas cookies, either?" she asked. "Because I haven't eaten since breakfast and I could really use a bite of something sweet. I have to eat a snack every three hours, or else I get this low blood sugar thing, and I really don't want to pass out on you again. If you don't have cookies, I'll—"

"Hang on." I filled the teakettle with water and set it on the stove, then dug through the pantry. I had a fuck ton of MREs stockpiled in there; maybe the nutrition bars would help with her blood sugar thing. "Here."

Maddie grabbed it from my hand, turning it over to read the label. "Soldier Fuel?"

"It's like a cookie. Closest thing I got, anyway. Look, it's chocolate. Just eat it and be happy."

"No problem. This looks... good." She tore open the wrapper and nibbled on the corner of the bar, trying not to make a face. "Hey, if by some miracle we find a way out of here tonight, you should come with me to

Christmas dinner! My family won't mind—the more the merrier. I mean, they don't even know *I'm* coming. And my mom makes this crazy feast, with turkey and ham, two kinds of mashed potatoes, three or four different salads, sweet potatoes with pecans... Well, my dad probably polished those off by now—they're his favorite. Oh! She also makes this amazing creamed spinach thing baked in a tree-shaped dish and decorated with little red tomatoes to look like—"

"Pass. Hard pass." I shook my head so fast I nearly gave myself whiplash. "I don't do Christmas. Don't do families either."

She opened her trap to say something else, but apparently thought better of it because she stuck the nutrition bar in her mouth instead, and the yammering finally ceased for a full thirty seconds. I could've sworn my ears were ringing. I'd almost forgotten what quiet actually sounded like.

But after two minutes without a word from the girl, I actually missed the sound of her voice. Something was obviously bugging her.

I'm going to regret this, but...

"Spill it, Cupcake."

"Spill what?"

"Whatever it is that miraculously stopped your gums from flapping." I pulled out the chair next to her, spun it around backward, and straddled it, leaning in close. "It's not like you."

Maddie finally smiled, and it lit up her whole damn face. I couldn't stop staring at her freckles. I wanted to count them. To kiss them. To peel off her clothes and find out if she had freckles anywhere else.

"It's just... okay," she said, the spot between her eyebrows crinkling. "Christmas is, like, *epic* in my family. My parents go all out. Costumes. Decorations. Enough lights to drain the power grid, enough food to feed a small country, presents galore, caroling—"

"Caroling? As in, you all sit around the fireplace singing Christmas songs to each other?" I grinned. It was like something right out of one of those fucking Hallmark movies. "Do you do that thing with the popcorn on a thread, too?"

"Yes on the singing, no on the popcorn. Popcorn is one of the things I'm allergic to. Also, I hate needles." She squeezed her eyes shut and did a full-bodied shiver. "Hate-hate-*hate* 'em."

I thought of the jagged white scar gouged into my right thigh. Hatchet wound, pre-wolf. I'd stitched myself up with a 1960s field kit and some duct tape in the middle of the Bolivian jungle after an opium kingpin's bodyguard got the drop on me, icing two of my best men in the ensuing fight.

Guess I won't be telling her that *story tonight.*

"Anyway," she said, "even if the storm breaks, *and* the phones come back online, *and* I can get a tow truck to come all the way out here, I'm already missing all the good stuff. And my sister and her family are leaving right after lunch tomorrow, so I might not even get to see my nieces and my new nephew, which is the whole reason I got the costume in the first place, and now I'm stuck here, and everything is..." She closed her eyes as the tears slipped out. "I'm sorry. I don't mean to sound ungrateful. It's just... it's been a tough couple of years. This year was supposed to be different."

Fuck. What was I supposed to say to that? I had no idea how to make her feel better, or why I even cared all of sudden. All I knew was that for some stupid-ass reason, I was missing that kid-on-Christmas smile of hers something fierce, and the whole thing was about to make me wolf out.

"Hey." I cupped her face in my big hands, wiping away the tears with my thumbs. "You'll get there. I can't promise you when, but if it's in my power to do it, I'll find a way."

When she finally opened her eyes, she was smiling again, and *damn* if it didn't get me all twisted up inside.

"Thanks," she said softly, curling her hands around my wrists. Her touch was electric, sending an instant message to my dick, which had been suspended in a state of perpetual hardness ever since she'd passed out in my arms. "You're not half bad when you drop that whole brooding, bad-boy thing."

The teakettle whistled, and I got up to brew the coffee, grateful for an excuse to put some distance between us. Another fifteen seconds up close like that, and I would've kissed her so hard it would've left a damn bruise.

"Brooding bad boy, huh?" I laughed. "Newsflash, Cupcake. It's called my natural state. Don't like it? There's the door."

Maddie finished up the nutrition bar in silence, then let out a sad little sigh.

"You know what?" she said. "I think I'll wait on the coffee. Do you mind if I take a shower and change? I can't seem to get warm."

I could think of about ten different ways to get her warm, and I *really* didn't want her to change out of those hot little stockings, but I shelved those fantasies for later.

"Yeah, no problem. Bathroom's upstairs, second door on the left. Try not to hog up all the hot water—the tank takes hours to refill."

"Fine." She got up from the table and unzipped the jacket I'd loaned her, revealing the tight, sparkly elf dress underneath. I was dying to know if those stockings went all the way up, or stopped at the tops of her thighs, leaving the tender curve of her ass exposed.

"You need any help getting out of that dress?" I asked. "It looks a little... tight."

Maddie rolled her eyes. "I'll be sure to let you know if I get stuck."

"Hey," I said with a wink. "Here to help."

She draped the jacket over the back of the chair, then crossed the kitchen to the stove, where I was still messing with the teakettle.

"Thanks, Hawke." She stood up on her tiptoes and pressed a kiss to my cheek, her perfect tits brushing my arm. "For everything."

My skin fucking *burned* with the fire of that chaste kiss. I could only imagine what it would be like to have her whole mouth, to shove my hands into her hair and pull her close, slide my tongue between her glossy pink lips as she moaned my name.

She held my gaze for a beat, her eyes darkening with something that looked a hell of a lot like desire, and I wondered whether she'd felt it, too—the slow-burn heat simmering between us, my sudden *need* to feel her skin, to taste her, to make her melt all over my cock.

But then she lowered her eyes and sighed, and I let it

go. It was for the best. She didn't need my kind of darkness in her life—not even for one night.

Maddie bit her lower lip, her cheeks heating with fresh color. "I should probably…"

"Yeah," I said. "You probably should."

I watched as she walked over to her suitcase by the door, her tight little ass bobbing beneath the poof of her ballerina dress like a pendulum, hypnotizing me with every step.

Fuck, it was gonna be a long night. And we hadn't even discussed sleeping arrangements yet.

Deep inside, the wolf growled to life once more, the need to claim her rising to the surface. If I let him out, even for one fucking minute, she'd be done for.

I couldn't let it happen. Not tonight. Not ever. Best to just keep things friendly and polite—no complications, no accidents. Let her shower in peace, then give her that coffee and maybe a hot meal, wish her a Merry Christmas, and fuck off to my bedroom alone, just like always.

HAWKE

I'd just poured another shot of that whiskey, trying to figure out what the hell to make for dinner for a girl with more allergies than I could fucking count, when the screaming started.

"Hawke!" she screeched, the sheer panic in her voice kicking my wolf's protective instincts into overdrive. "*Hawke!*"

It was all I could do not to shift on the spot. Bella and I bolted up the stairs, my heart pounding as I tried not to trip over the damn dog. When I got up there, I didn't bother knocking—just barged right on through the bathroom door.

"What happened?" I growled, barely keeping the wolf on lock. "You okay?"

"I'm fine," she said from behind the shower curtain,

her tone downshifting from panicked to annoyed. "God. You scared me."

"You're screaming like you're being attacked by a grizzly, and *I* scared *you*?"

"Hawke. There are no grizzlies in Colorado. Only black bears. And they're all hibernating this time of year, and even if they weren't, the chances of—"

"Maddie." I shoved my hands into my hair, trying to keep my brain from exploding like a damn land mine. "What do you *want*, woman?"

"I didn't think you could hear me."

"Well, I could."

"Sorry. Don't be mad, but... I kind of need a huge favor."

I swallowed hard, my heart rate kicking up again for a whole new reason.

If you need someone to soap up those beautiful tits, sign me the fuck up right now...

"I know I said I only needed the one bag from the trunk," she continued, "but I forgot something, and it's in a different bag."

I sighed into the steam billowing around me. *Of course it is.*

"It's super important."

Of course it is.

"I wouldn't ask otherwise."

Of course you wouldn't.

She slid open part of the shower curtain and poked her head out. "Please, Hawke?"

Those baby blues stood out against the slate-gray tile like pieces of the Colorado sky in summer. Her hair was slicked back, showing off the delicate curves of her face—high cheekbones, a thin nose that turned up at the tip, right over those luscious lips. Her ears stuck out a little, which only made her all the more fucking adorable.

Water streamed down her face, and when she raised a hand to wipe her eyes, I caught a flash of bare shoulder and collarbone that called to some deep, primal part of my soul.

Everything in me wanted to fucking bite her—not just the wolf, but the man, too. I wanted to yank that curtain right off the rings, jump in there, grab that juicy little ass in my hands and slam her against the tile, claiming that hot, slippery flesh with a single thrust that would leave her begging and gasping...

"Hawke?"

"What is it?" I snapped.

"You... totally spaced on me."

I closed my eyes and took a deep breath, steam filling my lungs. "I *meant*, what's so important that you wanna send me back out in a blizzard to fetch it like a trained lapdog?"

"Just... it's my... conditioner," she said awkwardly.

"There's shampoo and shit on the shelf in there. Use whatever you want."

"I can't. It's... it's a special conditioner that I have to use or my hair gets dry and brittle, and then it gets all frizzy and I can't do anything with it because it's naturally curly and the dry winter air makes everything worse, especially at altitude, and—"

"For fuck's sake, woman! Are you always this fucking annoying, or only on special occasions?"

She didn't answer.

I scrubbed a hand over my jaw, guilt needling my insides. *Might as well put my balls in a jar and hand 'em right over.*

"Fine. What do you need, Maddie?"

Her sigh of relief was audible, even over the sound of the water. "Thank you! Okay, in the car there's an attaché case, a roll-aboard, a personal carry-on, and a shoulder bag. I need the attaché. Wait, no—sorry. It's in the shoulder bag."

"You sure?"

"Yep. Shoulder bag. Definitely. The car keys are still in my coat pocket. Well, *your* coat pocket. Thanks again for—"

"I'll be right back. Sit tight."

"Yes sir," she quipped, and fuck if *that* didn't send my mind spiraling in all the wrong directions...

Ignoring the deep ache pulsating through my cock, I pulled the door shut and set out to fetching her shit.

***

Outside, the wind had only gotten more brutal, clawing at my face and hands as I stomped down to the end of the driveway. The car was piled high with fresh snow and a thin coating of ice—took me about ten minutes of scraping before I could even pop the damn trunk. Inside, I found three bags and a big, puffy coat the color of bubblegum. Another bag rested on the back seat.

What the fuck was the difference between a roll-aboard and an attaché case, anyway? Which one was the carry-on? Wait, no, it was the shoulder bag she'd asked for, right? Wasn't that the same thing as a purse? Fuck, they all looked exactly the same to me. I was five seconds from Hulk-smashing every damn one of them, along with the car and whatever bad Christmas mojo had brought this crazy-ass girl careening into my driveway in the first place.

Instead, I grabbed the coat and all four bags and tromped back up the driveway into the cabin, wondering how the fuck it was possible for a man to become pussy-whipped without getting any actual pussy.

Fucking hell.

I hauled the bags upstairs and knocked on the bathroom door like the good little man-servant I apparently was. "I couldn't tell them apart, so I brought them all."

"Come in," she said. "I can't hear you."

I opened the door and stuck my head in, not trusting myself to go any further than that without stripping out of my clothes and joining her, invitation or not. "I don't know which bag is which, so I brought them all."

"The shoulder bag is the small squishy one with the thick strap," she said. "Inside, there should be a smaller toiletry bag."

Bag inside of a bag. Right.

Why did chicks always cart around so much shit?

I tried to imagine her on assignment in some BFE shithole, traipsing up the side of a mountain with her unit. She'd need a herd of mules just to transport all this crap. It weighed more than she did.

Digging through the bag, I said, "I see a leopard-looking thing, a clear thing with more clear things inside, and a green thing with a black zipper."

"It's the green one," she said. "Just leave it on the counter for me."

"I'm standing right here, Maddie. I'll pass you the

damn conditioner. Just tell me what it looks like. A bottle? A tube? A—"

"Don't! I mean, it's fine." She popped her head out from behind the curtain again, her skin glowing pink. She looked so fresh-faced and innocent, I felt like I was corrupting her just by being in the same room as that pure, naked flesh. "Please just leave it, Hawke. I'll take care of it."

"Whatever." I dropped the bag on the counter, torn between wanting to throttle her and wishing like hell she'd ask for help soaping up after all.

If things kept on like this, I'd have blue balls until New Year's.

Assuming I still *had* balls.

"Hawke?" She poked her face out one last time, her smile genuine, making something in my chest twist. "Thank you. That was really sweet of you."

I nodded, all the air leaking out of my lungs. "Anytime, Cupcake."

Guess we solved that *fucking mystery, you pansy-ass, no-balls-havin' pussy.*

MADDIE

Wrapped up in a fluffy white towel, I rummaged through the green toiletry bag for my pills, double-checking each label to make sure I got the dosage right. This particular cocktail was a new combination, and I was still getting used to them, but they were the best ones yet. No mood swings, no tremors, and only a tiny bit of nausea when I didn't eat enough.

Best of all? No chipmunk face.

I lined them all up in my hand, counted them once more to be sure, then swallowed them with a handful of water from the sink. I was only off by an hour or so, but still. I couldn't afford to lose track like that again. What if I'd completely forgotten about them tonight? What if Hawke hadn't been able to get back into the car with all that snow?

I fisted my locket, whispering another ginormous *thank you.* I'd already had so many near-misses in my life, so many second chances... How many more would I get before I finally maxed out? Before the universe or God or whoever was in charge up there decided that keeping me alive was more trouble than it was worth?

Don't think like that, girl. You're doing fine. Totally fine.

Sucking in a deep breath, I capped the bottles and zipped everything back into the toiletry bag.

Right. *Medicine* bag was more like it.

I rolled my eyes. As if I'd really send someone out in a blizzard for conditioner, of all things. Hawke must've thought I was the silliest girl in the world.

Oh well. I'd gotten the pills—that was the important thing.

Normally, I would've taken the time to dry and flat-iron my hair, maybe dab on some lip gloss, but I wanted to get back downstairs to see if the phones were working yet so I could call my family and at least let them know I was in town. They'd probably been trying to call me all day, assuming I was celebrating Christmas alone in New York. I didn't want them to worry.

Yeah, girl. That's the reason you want to get downstairs. It has nothing to do with that sexy, tough-as-nails bad boy waiting for you in the kitchen wearing nothing but an apron and an oven mitt...

I laughed. Hawke was *so* not the apron-wearing type. And he most certainly wasn't down there *waiting* for me. If anything, he was probably hiding, afraid I'd talk him to death, or worse—send him outside again.

I still couldn't believe he'd actually gone out there and got all my bags.

What was his deal, anyway? One minute he was a gruff and hot-tempered jerk, and the next, he was the sweetest freaking guy I'd ever met.

Well, maybe *sweet* wasn't the right word. He'd definitely surprised me with moments of kindness and generosity, and despite his gruffness, I felt completely at ease around him, even when I was naked and vulnerable in the shower. But there was something dangerous about Hawke, too—a wild restlessness that simmered just beneath the surface, calling out to the same restlessness inside me.

I had a feeling he'd sensed it, too—whatever "it" was. He'd probably never admit it, but I could tell by the way he watched me, the way his eyes smoldered with barely contained passion, desperate for some kind of outlet.

Our paths were never meant to cross, but now that they had, I wanted to get to know him.

I wanted to... to touch him.

I wanted—I realized suddenly—to be utterly *taken* by him. And *that* thought shocked the hell out of me.

Sure, I'd always had little crushes and fantasies, every one of them ready to be conjured up in my mind at a moment's notice whenever my bed started to feel a little too cold and lonely. But I'd never felt such an intense physical pull toward a man—toward a total stranger—before. Especially not one whose default setting was Raging Jackass.

My whole body nearly burst into flames when he'd touched my face with those big hands and smoothed away my tears.

Crazy.

I hung my towel on the door hook and stood naked before the steamed-up mirror, my reflection a blur as I ran my hands down the front of my body. A vision slipped unbidden into my mind—Hawke standing behind me, his gaze fiery in the mirror, my breasts filling his hands as he stroked my nipples with those rough, calloused fingers...

Holy hell. Fifteen seconds of *that* naughty little daydream was enough to flood me with hot, molten desire that made me ache.

My thoughts were suddenly overrun with him: Hawke, gliding his hands along my curves. Hawke, pressing his hot mouth to the back of my neck, growling against my damp skin. Hawke, fisting his cock and ordering me to part my thighs for him. Hawke, bending me over the sink and taking *everything* I had to offer.

I bet he'd know *just* what he was doing, too.

I had a steady boyfriend in college—my first and only lover—but he'd always treated me like a glass doll. He honestly believed that sex might kill me, even on my healthiest days, and he didn't trust me to know my own limits. No matter how often I tried to experiment, to push things a little farther in the bedroom, our sex life never rose above lukewarm. Adequate, maybe. Comfortable and safe. But not wild. Not passionate.

Hawke Stevens? That man didn't know the *meaning* of comfortable and safe. The way he spoke, the way he carried himself, the cocky attitude, the rock-hard body... everything about him was aggressive, commanding, and hot as hell.

And he's probably as fierce and demanding in the bedroom as he is out of it...

A rush of heat washed through me once more, and I closed my eyes, wishing he was still in here with me, glaring at me through the steam, a storm brewing in his intense gray eyes...

I was *this* close to calling his name and asking for a *different* sort of favor this time...

No. No freaking way.

Guys like Hawke Stevens came with red flags so big and glaring you could spot them from the International Space Station, and I'd watched too many of my girlfriends go up in flames for ignoring those exact kinds of warning signs. Didn't matter how damn hot he was—I would *not* be adding my name to the list of the scorched and the scorned tonight.

I sighed and opened my eyes, accepting my fate. In the epic battle between protecting the heart and satisfying the vag, the heart had—once again—emerged victorious.

I needed to get dressed. Pronto.

I dug out a clean bra and panties from my suitcase, then tugged them on with a pair of yoga pants and a thermal Christmas shirt decorated with gingerbread cookies. The shirt had three small red buttons at the top, which I fastened all the way up to my neck.

When I got back downstairs, fresh and clean and *more* than ready to forget about my inappropriate daydreams, I was greeted by a sight even more shocking than my naughty apron-and-oven-mitt fantasy.

Hawke was cooking Christmas dinner.

MADDIE

I t smells amazing in here," I said, inhaling the aroma of sautéed veggies and something rich and decadent as I joined Hawke and Bella in the kitchen. A beet-and-orange salad was already on the table, along with bottled waters and a fresh mug of coffee, steam curling off the top.

"Coffee's ready," Hawke said, not yet glancing my way. He was standing at the sink, a yellow-and-white checkered dishtowel draped over his shoulder, his back to me as he drained a pot of cooked pasta. I took a second to admire the view, dragging my eyes across his broad shoulders and down his back, the curves of his muscles well-defined even underneath the gray hoodie. Both sleeves were pushed up to reveal tattooed forearms, thick and muscular and perfect for pinning me down...

Pull yourself together, train wreck! Red flags, remember? Heart before vag? We talked about this! You're taking a firm anti-Hawke stance for the rest of this disastrous holiday. Non-negotiable. Got it?

"So, you know how to cook?" I asked, a little too brightly.

"Nope. But since I gave the head chef the week off, you're outta luck." He turned to look at me over his shoulder, his smirk changing into a genuine smile when he saw me—probably the first real one he'd offered all night. It felt like a Christmas present.

"Cute shirt," he said, his eyes glittering. "Makes me wish I had some actual gingerbread cookies for you."

My heart fluttered. It freaking fluttered. And no, not in a medical emergency sort of way. This was a full-on, five-alarm, bad-boy-induced flutter that did *not* bode well for my so-called firm anti-Hawke stance.

"I thought you lived on Soldier Fuel bars," I said, massaging my chest and willing my heart to behave itself, like, *hey, jerkface! I'm trying to save you here! A little cooperation would be nice!*

"Only in combat situations." He set the pasta pot back on the stove and checked on the veggies sizzling away on another burner. "For instance, when I'm too hungover to go shopping."

"Guess I showed up on the right day, then, because this looks delicious." I gathered my damp hair into one hand and leaned over the stove to investigate. "I *love* pasta."

"I know you're allergic to a bunch of shit, so I kept it pretty basic. Fusilli. Sautéed spinach and mushrooms. Alfredo." He lifted a wooden spoon to his lips and sampled the sauce, letting out a satisfied moan that made my mouth water—and not from the succulent aroma filling up the kitchen. "Here. Tell me what you think."

Cupping his hand beneath my chin, Hawke tipped the spoon into my mouth, watching intently as I licked the excess from my lips and swallowed. It was so rich and creamy that one taste had my stomach grumbling in anticipation.

"You made this from scratch?" I asked.

"Hey, I don't fuck around when it comes to Alfredo." He released my chin and dipped the spoon back into the pot, taking another sample for himself. "Think it needs more salt?"

"Nope. It's perfect."

"Yeah, you're right." He smacked his lips together and set the spoon on a small dish off to the side, wiping his hands on the towel. "Have a seat. Sauce needs to simmer about ten more minutes, then I just need to toss the spinach in with the mushrooms and we're in business."

Bella followed me to the table in the breakfast nook, her nails clicking on the hardwood floor. The moment I sat down, she put her head in my lap.

"Hey!" Hawke snapped his fingers and pointed at the dog. "We talked about this, Bells. You don't put your head in a woman's lap without an invitation."

"Aww, she's fine. Such a good girl." I scratched behind her ears until the dog was putty in my hands, her tongue lolling out, her eyes half-closed. Bella's infinite affection reminded me of my old canine companion, Turkey. "Aren't you, baby? What's a nice girl like you doing with a grumpy old man like Hawke, anyway?"

The grunt that passed for Hawke's laugh echoed across the kitchen, but before he could retaliate with one of his smart-ass comments, a gust of wind whipped against the cabin, making the lights flicker.

"Oh shit," he said.

"What does that mean?" I asked.

"Nothing good."

"Don't you have a generator?"

"Yep. But it's—"

There was a hiss, and a pop, and everything went black.

"—broke," he finished. "I'm waiting on a part. Fuck."

I sighed. "Does this mean Soldier Fuel is back on the menu?"

"Not a chance, Cupcake." Hawke turned off the electric burners and covered the pots. "You're getting a proper Christmas dinner tonight, blizzard and electrical failures be damned. We'll just have to improvise."

Undeterred by the setback, he rummaged around in the pantry and pulled out a bunch of outdoor gear—three small metal camping stoves, lightweight pots, fuel canisters, half a dozen emergency candles, a lantern, and a box of matches.

I lit everything up and arranged the candles on the table and countertop, then watched as Hawke transferred the Alfredo into two smaller pots, hooked up the stoves to the fuel, and set the flames to simmer. He dumped the mushrooms into a third pot and instructed me to keep stirring while he added fresh spinach, a handful at a time.

"Wow." I was beyond impressed. If this had happened at my place, we'd be going for takeout. "So you're one of those nutjob preppers, obviously."

Hawke scoffed. "Nothing wrong with being prepared for an emergency."

"Says the man who let his generator die in the middle of winter."

"Oh, that's pretty rich," he teased, "coming from a girl who treks through the high country dressed like Santa's little hooker."

"Oh my god, rude!" I smacked his arm, letting my hand linger. His thick muscles undulated beneath my fingertips.

Hawke caught my gaze and held it, those flint-gray eyes sparking dangerously in the candlelight. Heat pooled low in my belly, just waiting for him to make a move—to turn that one little spark into a raging inferno, burning my earlier reservations to ash.

Do it. Just kiss me. Drop everything else and kiss me, right now, before I spontaneously combust...

"We... better sit down," he finally said, his deep, gruff voice intimate in the soft light. "Dinner's ready, and Alfredo's no good when it's cold."

Nodding, I removed my hand and reclaimed my seat at the table, and the moment between us passed, leaving a still-simmering tension in the air that did nothing to cool my rapidly overheating insides.

"Sorry there ain't a fancy dish in the shape of a *tree*," Hawke said, rolling his eyes, "but hopefully the food still tastes good."

He put everything into serving bowls and loaded up

the table with a feast fit for kings and queens. Tree dish or not, I was starving and beyond grateful. I couldn't wait to dive in.

From an unlabeled bottle on the counter, Hawke poured himself a glass of dark, amber liquid, then said, "You good with water and coffee, or do you want something that'll put a little hair on your chest?"

"I don't need hair on my chest. And I thought you weren't keen on sharing that whiskey, anyway?"

"Not usually, but hey. It's Christmas, we're about to enjoy a home-cooked meal, and you're wearing a shirt covered in gingerbread cookies. I'll make an exception."

My cheeks heated under his gaze. "Thanks anyway, but I'm good. I don't drink."

"Ever?" Hawke raised an eyebrow, but I wasn't in the mood to elaborate.

"This looks incredible, Hawke. Seriously." I reached for the beet salad and spooned a pile of it onto my plate. "Thank you."

"Yeah, well." Bringing his bottle and glass to the table, Hawke sat down across from me and shrugged. "Gotta eat, right? Don't get sentimental on me."

"Oh, I won't get sentimental on you. I won't even get sentimental *near* you. I hear sentimentality is highly contagious."

Hawke tried to shoot me a tough-guy glare, but he

couldn't keep a straight face. Pointing at me with his fork, he said, "Just pass me that salad and don't get cute. Well, any *more* cute."

"No sentimentality. No cuteness. Hmm. I'm going to need a list to keep all your rules straight."

His grin widened, his eyes sparkling with dark mischief. The kind that had me thinking those wicked, red-hot thoughts all over again—thoughts I *really* hoped he couldn't read.

"Or," he said, his voice turning as dark as his eyes, "you could *break* all my rules and deal with the punishment."

MADDIE

Permanent blushing? Check.

Damp panties? Check.

Wicked, uncontrollable thoughts involving tattooed forearms and a filthy mouth? Checkety check check check.

They were just symptoms, I told myself. Temporary symptoms of some strange new condition I'd caught in his presence—a condition that would pass the moment the storm broke and I could return to my normal life.

But for now, I'd just have to learn to manage it. Because unlike all the other conditions in my life, I was pretty sure no one made a pill for Hawke Stevens.

We managed to get through the salad course without further incident. After clearing away the small plates, Hawke served up heaping portions of the main course, smothering everything with that mouthwatering Alfredo sauce.

Out beyond the cozy cabin, the wind screamed through the high peaks, coating the windows with ice and snow as Hawke and I enjoyed the meal in companionable silence. Bella's nails clicked softly as she paced around the table in search of scraps, the fire in the living room crackling, everything about the moment filling me with a sense of peace and contentment I hadn't thought possible just a handful of hours earlier.

Despite his best efforts to be a total Grinch—a strong, hot, filthy one, but a Grinch nevertheless—Hawke had given me a decent Christmas dinner after all.

I reached across the small table and squeezed his fingers. He flinched at the touch, but didn't pull away, and I left my hand there, not quite ready to let him go.

"What's up?" He slid his thumb across my knuckles, a tiny gesture that made me shiver. "You've gone quiet on me again."

"That's because I'm eating. Stick something in my mouth, and it'll shut me right up."

Hawke arched a playful brow. "Good to know."

"I didn't mean... *Anyway*." I pulled my hand away and lowered my eyes to my coffee mug, cheeks on fire once again. "Everything was delicious. Thank you,

Hawke. Your dirty mind aside, you actually made my Christmas Eve not so sucky."

He laughed, loud and gravelly, a sound I wanted to capture and bottle for the next stormy night—for a time when I'd be long gone from this place. From him.

"I aim to please, Cupcake."

I met his gaze as he raised his glass in salute, then sipped his whiskey. When he lowered the glass again, he was watching me with a look I couldn't decipher, another smile twitching at the corners of his mouth.

"What?" I asked. "Why are you staring at me like that?"

Hawke reached forward and tugged on one of my corkscrew curls, pulling it straight, then releasing it like a spring. It was mostly dry now, but wild and untamed since I hadn't bothered to style it.

"Your hair is *mad* curly."

"I know. I usually straighten it, but—"

"What? Fuck that." He looped another lock around his finger, his knuckles brushing my cheek. "I like it just like this."

"Really?"

"Really."

Warmth spread across my chest. "What else do you like?"

Hawke laughed again, releasing my hair and settling back into his chair. "Um..."

"I mean," I rushed to clarify, "like, what else do you enjoy doing? For fun. Or work. Or... whatever. Okay, you *know* what I mean, Hawke. Does everything have to be about sex with you?"

Oh my god, stop talking. Shove something else in your mouth and stop talking right now.

"Please, do go on." A wicked grin lit up Hawke's face, candlelight reflecting in his eyes as he basked in the glow of my endless mortification. "What were you saying about sex with me?"

"I'm just... I'm just trying to make conversation. Like regular people. You know? You tell me something interesting about you, I reciprocate, we progress from total strangers to... slightly less strange?"

Hawke took another sip of his whiskey, then sighed. "Unfortunately, I ain't that interesting."

I glanced around the cabin, taking in the open floor plan, the timber-framed architecture, the hardwood floors, the plush area rugs, the custom-built stone fireplace, the huge flatscreen, the security TVs mounted in the kitchen. "Pretty sweet setup you've got here for such a boring guy. What do you do for a living?"

"Mostly I sit around all day and scratch my balls.

Watch a little porn. Drink myself into a stupor. Good times."

"They pay you for that?"

"Not anymore." He flashed his trademarked panty-melting smirk. "I'm retired."

I narrowed my eyes at him over the rim of my coffee mug. "Yeah, right. What are you, forty?"

"Thirty-four, smartass."

"What kind of work lets you retire that young?"

"Eh, this and that."

"Sounds like code for something shady."

Hawke grabbed my fork and speared the last lonely mushroom on my plate, lifting it to my lips. "It's code for shut your mouth and finish your dinner before I spank you and send you to bed early."

Holy hell.

My stomach dropped to the floor, my thighs clenching together at the sound of his deep voice, his teasing threat.

Joking or not, the idea of Hawke spanking me sent shivers racing up and down my spine.

It felt naughty. Forbidden.

Hot.

I was pretty sure my nipples were now on full display, distorting the poor little gingerbread people.

The way Hawke stared at my mouth wasn't helping matters.

I swallowed and grabbed my water, chasing down the mushroom with a big gulp.

"Your turn." Hawke set down the fork and leaned back in his chair. "Based on the sheer amount of crap you packed into that car, I'm guessing you don't live close by. Or you're even more high-maintenance than I thought."

I shifted in my chair, attempting to relieve some of the pressure building up between my thighs, but it was useless.

"I grew up in Denver," I said. "My family's all still here. But I moved to New York for college and ended up staying. And unlike you, I'm *not* a retired, ball-scratching, alcoholic, porn-watcher. I actually have to work for a living."

"*Pffft.* Whose fault is that? Sounds to me like someone needs to reevaluate her life choices."

"Nah, I love my work. I have my own business designing and building websites. I set my own schedule, my clients are awesome, and I get to be creative and analytical at the same time. Dream job—seriously."

"That's the kind of work you can do from anywhere, though. Why would you pick the most crowded, expensive city in the country? Not to mention a prime target for all sorts of shit you can't even imagine." Hawke shook his head and leaned forward, his face turning grim and serious. "Tell you this much, Cupcake. Shit goes down? New York is the *last* place you wanna be."

"Who's the cupcake now, tough guy?" I rolled my eyes. "Shit goes down there every day. I could tell you stories you wouldn't *believe*. And it's not *that* expensive—I have a roommate."

"Yeah? What's her story?" Hawke drained his whiskey, then poured himself another shot. "Tell me it involves pillow fights, mutual showers, and walking around the apartment naked, otherwise I honestly don't care because I'm sticking with my version."

I rolled my eyes. "*His* story is he's an architect. I don't see him all that much because he works even more than I do."

"*His*?" The muscles along Hawke's jaw ticked. "Your roommate is a dude?"

"That's how he identifies, yes."

"So I assume you're banging this fancy-ass architect?"

"Hawke!" I waited for him to apologize, but of course he wouldn't. Diplomacy was not part of Hawke's skill set. "For your *nosey* information, no. Derrick and I aren't together—not like that. I don't even know him all that well, honestly. It was a Craigslist thing."

"He's never made a move?"

"No."

"Gay?"

"I don't know. I mean, I've never seen him with a guy, and he's definitely brought women home before, so—"

"Women. He's hooked up with women, but not you?"

"We're just... we're not into each other. He's—*what*? Why are you looking at me like that?"

"You live with a dude who's not gay and you think he's not spending every waking moment trying to figure out how to get into your pants?" Hawke laughed until his eyes watered. "You're too sweet for your own good, Maddie Lockwood."

"Believe it or not, some people have evolved beyond their baser instincts. Look at us, right? We're sitting here having a nice dinner, finally having a real conversation. *You're* not trying to get in my pants."

Hawke raised that maddening eyebrow again and fixed me with a hard glare that made my breath catch. "You sure about that?"

This conversation was rapidly going off the rails. I couldn't handle those intense eyes, not when I was still imagining what his hands would feel like smacking my bare ass. Not when he was playing with my curls and messing with my head and asking rude questions about my sex life.

"I invited you into my home," Hawke went on, his deep voice vibrating straight through my chest. "Checked out your car. Fetched your luggage. Let you use up all my hot water. Cooked you my secret recipe Alfredo sauce. This is A-game, panty-melting shit right here, Cupcake."

My mouth went dry, heart jackhammering inside my chest, my lungs just short of stalling out on me...

And it was only going to get worse.

Hawke was a *master* at this game, and now that he'd seen how easy it was to get under my skin, he wasn't going to let up. He was like a predator in the wild, stalking me, homing in on my weaknesses, wearing me down until I finally admitted defeat.

Well, I had some news for him. Maddie Lockwood might blush, she might squirm, she might completely freak out on the inside, but she did *not* admit defeat.

Hawke wanted to play naughty little games? Fine. I could play too.

Just as hard. Just as dirty.

MADDIE

It was a bold move—one I never would've attempted if I thought I'd actually see him again after tonight —but I was ready to fight fire with fire.

Leaning back in my chair, I loosened the tie on my yoga pants and slipped a hand inside, closing my eyes and pretending to give myself a thorough investigation.

Oh, *damn.*

I wasn't surprised at how hot I was, at how wet; I'd been in a constant state of arousal since he'd first stepped onto that porch with his glistening abs on full display. But I certainly wasn't expecting the barest brush of my own fingers to send a jolt of pleasure buzzing across my every nerve.

My breath caught on a gasp, and I yanked my hand out of my pants and forced out a laugh.

"Sorry, tough guy," I said, attempting a deadpan, probably failing. "My panties are still intact, completely unmelted. Guess your A-game's a little rusty. You should probably get out more—brush up on those pre-game skills."

When I finally met his gaze again, Hawke was glaring at me hard, his chest heaving, fist clamped so tight around his glass, I thought it might shatter.

"Don't... don't do that again," he ground out, anger flashing in those stormy eyes.

Heat rushed to my cheeks, and this time it wasn't because he'd gotten me worked up. No, this was the heat of shame. Raw, uncut shame. I felt like a naughty schoolgirl who'd just gotten busted cheating on a test.

"I'm sorry," I whispered, unable to hold his gaze. "I didn't—"

"You done?" Hawke shoved his chair back and stood up to clear the dishes from the table, all the levity and camaraderie vanishing in a blink.

"I... yes. I'm done." I closed my eyes and willed the floor to open up and swallow me whole.

Without another word, Hawke finished clearing the table. Filled the sink with hot, soapy water. Scraped every last dish into the compost bin. Refilled Bella's food and water bowls.

And still—*still*—the stupid floor remained unmoved

by my plea, leaving me there to suffer in silent, paralyzed horror.

I couldn't believe I actually thought I could beat him at his own game. Instead, all I'd done was mortify myself and seriously piss him off in the process.

Or worse—disgust him. His vibe was so stormy, so angsty, it was hard to get an accurate read. All I knew for sure was that the man was *not* happy with my little performance.

God, what was I thinking? Touching myself at the dinner table? I didn't even know him!

After wiping down the table without meeting my eyes even once, Hawke got to work scrubbing the dishes.

It felt like an hour passed. A day. And then...

"You okay?" he finally said, the unexpected sound of his voice crashing through the tense silence and making me jump. "Awfully quiet over there again, and there's no food in your mouth so I know it can't be—"

"Stop. Stop!" I hopped up from my chair, nearly tripping over poor Bella, who yelped and darted into the living room. "I mean... the dishes," I said awkwardly. "Let me take care of the dishes. I don't mind."

I joined him at the sink and pushed up my gingerbread sleeves.

Elbows-deep in the sudsy water, Hawke didn't

budge. "It's fine, Maddie. I've got it. You just go relax or... whatever it is you need to do."

"No, I'm serious. You cooked. I'll wash." I dipped my hands into the hot, slippery water, fingers gliding down the length of his tattooed forearms in search of the sponge. I couldn't help it; I *had* to touch him, even if it was just for a second.

God, he felt so good. So solid and strong.

Instead of pulling back like I expected, Hawke turned his hands over in the water and laced our fingers together. A million electric tingles raced up my arms, across my shoulders, and down my spine, straight to my core.

"You're trembling," he said softly, tracing my skin with his thumbs, slow and gentle. Mesmerizing.

I let out a soft breath, everything in me vibrating with need as our fingers continued their erotic dance under the water, skin sliding against skin, my shoulder brushing against his arm as I leaned in closer, seeking his warmth.

"I'm..." Hawke sighed, and though I still hadn't met his eyes, I could feel his gaze sweeping down the side of my face, my skin heating in its wake. "I'm not the man you think I am, Maddie."

"You have no idea what I'm thinking," I whispered.

Frankly, neither did I. I was so far out of my comfort

zone, so far beyond any rational thing I'd ever done in my life, I hardly recognized myself. With every flirty innuendo, every joke, every touch, I was charting brand-new territory.

But something about Hawke had worked its way deep under my skin, and in the hours since my ill-fated arrival, that something had smoldered into an aching need that pulsed red-hot between my thighs, begging for a release that only Hawke could give me.

I'd never felt this way around a man before—so reckless, so out of control.

It scared the hell out of me.

And I *liked* it. *Really* liked it.

I finally found the courage to tilt my head and meet his gaze. The flickering candlelight threw shadows across his face, sharpening the angles, darkening the stubble across his well-defined jaw. There was something savage and beautiful in his eyes—a dare, a warning, maybe a little of both.

When he finally spoke again, his voice was dark and menacing. "Don't you *dare* start something with me you can't finish."

I wanted to tell him I wouldn't. To confess that I'd been fantasizing about him all night. To promise that I would absolutely, positively see it all the way through if only he'd give me a chance. If only he'd cross the line he kept dancing around and finally freaking *kiss* me.

But instead, as I gazed into those wild eyes, my heart pounding, my chest rising and falling with every terrified breath, his evergreens-and-cinnamon scent stirring me into a frenzy, I shrunk inside, confidence vanishing once again.

Who was I kidding? There was nothing wrong with Hawke's A-game. He was a total pro, so confident and commanding and sure. Next to him, I was every bit the little girl my gingerbread shirt suggested.

And I was totally out of my league.

"I... I'm sorry," I muttered. "I guess I just got a little carried away and... Yeah. I'm sorry."

Shame burned once more through my chest, and I released his hands and turned back toward the table, looking for more dishes to gather, a dog to pet, another candle to light, *anything* to distract me from my self-induced humiliation—an ache that was only magnified by the pulsing-hot need still coursing through my body.

In that moment, all I wanted to do was march out the door, raise my arms to the heavens, and let the bitter winter wind sweep me away.

I was giving up—a thing I *never* did—and that pissed me right off.

I pressed a hand to my chest, the locket warming

against my skin, finally snapping me out of my pity party.

I'd spent so many years of my life being afraid, so many years playing it safe, so many years apologizing for things that I had no control over. And I was tired of it. Tired of shrinking away. Tired of living my life as if one stiff breeze—or the rejection of a hot, grumpy Grinch, for that matter—could take me down for good.

So no, I *didn't* want to be swept away by the winter wind.

I wanted to be swept away by *him*.

"Hawke, wait." I turned back to him and met his eyes again, giving him a fiery glare of my own. Maybe I didn't have the confidence to put my feelings into words, to make all those confessions or promises out loud, but I wanted him to know *exactly* where I stood. What I wanted. What I hoped he wanted too.

I'd just have to show him.

He was still at the sink, and before I could overthink it again, I closed the distance between us and slid my arms around him from behind, resting my cheek against his back. He stiffened in my hold, but didn't pull away, so I slid my hands down across his abs, then lower, brushing across the front of his jeans.

He was rock hard.

For me.

I cupped him through the jeans, feeling the full, delicious weight of him in my hand, my core flooding with unchecked desire as I imagined his massive cock thrusting into my flesh, again and again and again...

"What are you *doing*, Maddie? Jesus *fuck*." Hawke tried to shake me off, tried to resist, but he was already groaning at my touch, his hips rocking as I slowly rubbed him. When he finally turned to look at me over his shoulder, he was smiling again, but it wasn't his usual smart-ass, nothing-can-touch-me smirk.

It was the grin of a wolf, hungry and desirous, ready to devour its prey.

In another low growl that sent goosebumps skittering across my skin, he said, "You *really* shouldn't have done that."

And if there was one thing I'd learned in our short time together, it was this:

Hawke Stevens never said a thing unless he absolutely, positively meant it.

HAWKE

In one fluid motion, I jerked my hands out of the sink, whipped around, and grabbed Maddie good and tight. She gasped in surprise, her blue eyes glinting with a hint of fear, but that was too damn bad. My sweet, innocent little Christmas elf had had tempted the wolf inside, and now that the beast was fully awake, there'd be *no* putting him down.

Not until we fucking *claimed* her.

Before she could utter another word, I spun her around and pushed her against the countertop, my arms a cage around her upper body, my raging-hard cock digging into her round, perfect ass.

Fucking hell, she was hot as sin.

Lowering my face to the soft curve where her neck met her shoulder, I inhaled the scent of her skin, like warm vanilla and nutmeg, like the last bit of wholesome sweetness in a world where everything else had turned to ash.

Slowly, enjoying every torturous moment, I dragged my mouth to her ear and nipped at the fleshy lobe, unleashing another gasp from her lips.

"Listen up and listen good," I growled. "Because I'm warning you—we cross this line tonight? There's *no* going back."

I didn't like head games, and if that's all this was, I needed to know now so I could toss her out on her ass for good.

"I don't want to go back." Maddie's voice was clear and certain, full of some new fire. "I want *you*, Hawke."

"You don't know *what* you want, Cupcake." I let out a dark chuckle, enjoying the way the fine hairs on her neck stood on end as my breath whispered across her skin. "Not yet. But oh, you will. By the time I'm done with you, you'll be *begging* for it, again and again, until you're so sore you can't even fucking *walk*."

Another gasp. Another tremor rippling through her body. Another wave of heat cresting between us, making my cock *ache* with need.

Burying my face in those wild red curls, I forced her legs apart with my thigh, grinding into her pussy from behind. The layers of fabric between us did nothing to camouflage her desire.

She was hot. And wet. *So* fucking wet for me.

"Hawke," she moaned, my name a desperate plea as she arched her hips and rode my leg.

I slid a soapy-wet hand inside the front of her shirt, cupping one of her tits over the lace bra. It fit perfectly in my palm, pert nipple rising stiff at my touch.

Fuck, I wanted her in my mouth. I wanted to bite and tease that perfect little peak, to suck on it until it hurt, until she cried out with pain and pleasure both.

"I want you," she said again, her voice thick with pleasure.

"You broke *all* my rules tonight, Cupcake," I breathed, pinching her nipple, rolling it between my thumb and index finger as she slowly rocked against my thigh. "So this ain't about what you *want*. It's about what you're gonna get."

"What... what am I getting?" she muttered, nearly breathless now.

"Spanked. Fucked. And thoroughly wrecked."

I pressed my thigh harder against her center, making her whimper.

"First," I warned, "I'm tearing off these pants and smacking that sweet little ass until it's so red you'll make

Rudolph the fucking Reindeer jealous. After that? When your greedy little pussy is dripping wet and you're damn near *delirious* with need? I'm gonna make you *beg* for it. Beg me to touch you, beg me to taste you, beg me to let you come all over my tongue." I leaned closer once more, lips brushing her ear, a depraved growl rumbling up through my chest. "So think *real* hard about what you say next, 'cause I'm only asking once: are we crossing this line tonight? Or am I walking away right the fuck now?"

"Yes," she breathed, a dark flush creeping up her neck. "Yes to crossing the line. *All* the lines. Please just... just don't ever stop touching me."

"Ever?" I laughed, dark and low. "Just how far are we taking this, Cupcake?"

"I don't... I don't care. As far as you want." As if to underscore the point, she ground down against my thigh and let out a soft moan.

I closed my eyes and bit back a curse. *As far as you want...* Girl didn't know she was playing with *serious* fire. And if I wasn't careful, sweet little Maddie Lockwood—with her freckles and curls and ridiculous gingerbread cookie shirt—might get hurt.

The thought of it had my wolf raging inside, ready to smash something.

"Gingerbread," I whispered, opening my eyes and

blowing out a breath, trying to keep my wolf—and my raging cock—in check.

"Ginger... *what*?"

"That's your safe word," I said. "Anything gets too intense, you say the word and we're done."

"But I—"

"What's the word, Maddie?"

"You're serious."

"Say it. Say it right fucking now, so I know you've got it."

"Fine," she huffed. "Gingerbread. But I'm not *saying* it, saying it. Just... just this one time. Following your orders."

A slow grin slid across my face, and I nuzzled the back of her neck again. "Good girl."

My cock was practically screaming at me to tear off her clothes and bury myself in her tight little ass, but now that I had her here, willing and eager, I wasn't about to cash in on some two-and-a-half minute fuckfest. No way.

Didn't matter how badly I wanted to come right the fuck *now*.

Didn't matter how badly my wolf was tearing me apart inside, desperate to bite her. To mark her. To make her ours.

Maddie was my beautiful, innocent, perfect little

Christmas cupcake—the kind made to be savored all night long, slowly and deliberately.

One hand still massaging her breast, I ran the other hand up the back of her neck, fisting those wild, red curls. Her hair was so damn soft, cold and damp underneath where it hadn't completely dried. I leaned in close again, inhaling the scent of her exposed neck, sweetness and heaven.

"You have no idea how fucking sexy you are," I whispered, brushing my lips against her nape. "I've been hard for you ever since I opened the door and found you standing on my porch in those candy-cane tights."

"Stockings," she panted. "They're... they're stockings. Tights go all the way up."

"I see." Still fisting her hair, I released her breast and trailed my fingers down inside the waistband of her pants, skimming the silky-soft skin of her stomach, down to the top edge of her panties. I rubbed the lace between my thumb and forefinger, memorizing the feel of it on my skin. I fucking *had* to—after tonight, this fantasy would get me through a decade of lonely nights, and I wanted every detail, every texture, every scent permanently seared into my memory.

"You were right," I said. "These panties *are* still intact. That's no good." I jerked the lace upward, yanking it hard against her clit, then releasing it and sliding my fingers inside. Gliding over her bare, smooth-as-silk skin, I wondered if she'd recently shaved.

Very recently. Like... in my shower recently.

The thought of it sent me into overdrive.

"Did you shave tonight, Maddie?" I whispered, my heart slamming into my ribs, lungs fighting for breath as the images of her wet, naked flesh tumbled through my mind unbidden. "Did you use my razor to shave this pussy bare for me?"

"I... I... yes. I saw it on the ledge with your shampoo and I just... I... I'm sorry."

"Not as sorry as you're about to be, you naughty, naughty girl." I skimmed a finger over her clit, heat radiating from her body in waves as I stroked her with a light touch, driving her fucking mad.

"Hawke, that's... *Holy snowballs,* that's so..." She trailed off on a soft moan. Another shiver rolled through her limbs, her body responding to my every touch.

"Does that feel good, Cupcake?"

"So... so good."

"Are you sure?" I asked, my mouth against her ear. I dipped my fingers lower, teasing her outer lips and pulling back again, dragging the hot slickness back over her clit. She quivered in my arms, melting like butter at my touch. I couldn't wait to slide my cock inside of her, take her hard and deep. My balls ached, heavy with need, the wolf howling inside like a crazed beast, but I wasn't ready for the main course—not by a long shot. "Or would you rather touch yourself again? Maybe you're better at this than I am. Looked like you knew *exactly* what you were doing before."

"No, I..." She shook her head, her curls brushing my mouth, hitting me with another wave of her addicting vanilla scent. "I wasn't... I was just trying to... I—"

"*Maybe* you were just trying to tease me. Just trying to make me jealous, wishing I could replace your soft, delicate little fingers with my hot, filthy mouth."

"Oh, god." She let out a gasp, arching her body to steal more friction from my touch, but I wasn't about to give in.

"God won't help you tonight, Cupcake. Even if he could hear you scream, I'm pretty sure he'd take my side." I pulled out abruptly, grinding my cock against her ass once more. "*No* man likes to be teased."

"I wasn't teasing, I swear. I was just—"

"What? What were you *just*?"

"I—I was—"

"Show me." I grabbed her hand and forced it down the front of her panties, urging her fingers into a slow, circular motion against her clit.

She gasped again but didn't resist, and I pushed her

farther, using two of my fingers to guide one of hers deep inside.

Damn, did she feel good.

So slippery. So soft. So hot.

"Show me how you touch yourself," I commanded. "Show me what you do when you're all alone in your bed in New York City, desperate to drown out the lights and the sirens, desperate to make yourself shatter."

I kept my touch light, urging Maddie to take control, just this once. Just so I could see how she liked it. So I could fucking *feel* it.

"That's it," I murmured as she took over. "Just like that. You're gonna show me *exactly* how you'll fuck yourself when you're back home remembering what I did to you tonight. Because from here on out, I *know* you'll be thinking of me every time you touch this red-hot pussy, won't you?"

"Yes. Hawke, I... *Yes.*"

"Good girl."

She whimpered again, slipping another finger inside herself, deeper and deeper, then drawing back, only to plunge inside once more, then out, then in again, an erotic dance that slowly melted away the last of her shy, sweet embarrassment.

And made my fucking head spin harder than Kiko's illicit booze.

Letting her take over completely, I withdrew my fingers and dropped to my knees, gently rolling the yoga pants down her hips, sliding them off her legs to reveal the most shapely plum of an ass I'd ever seen. A white lace thong barely covered the twin mounds, the flimsy scrap of fabric pulling tight as she continued to stroke and plunder, making herself so wet, I could fucking *hear* it.

"Mmm. Such a nice ass for such a naughty girl." I buzzed my lips along the crease where the curve of one cheek met her upper thigh, flicking my tongue across the center as I blazed a trail from one thigh to the other, making her hips jolt against the countertop. "But unlike Santa, I don't give a *fuck* about naughty or nice. You're getting spanked either way."

Maddie gasped, but the arch of her hips told me she wanted every minute of it, as hard and as dirty as I wanted to give it to her.

Fuck, the scent of her desire was so damn overpowering, so damn enticing, I had to fight to remain in my human form.

Maddie Lockwood made me feel like a fucking *animal*. Like I'd been born the feral wolf, and the human body I now inhabited was nothing more than a temporary shift. A temporary mistake.

Biting back another growl, I rubbed one of her soft

globes, then the other. Then I raised my hand and smacked her ass with a crack that startled Bella from her snooze in the living room. The dog yelped and high-tailed it upstairs, but Maddie only moaned, crazy red hair cascading down her back, her head falling forward like a rag doll as she gave herself a thorough fingerbanging. I smacked her ass again, then ghosted my palm over the rapidly pinkening flesh, soothing the sting.

"Hawke!" she cried out, her legs trembling. "I'm going to—"

Crack!

"No, you're not," I demanded, my palm radiating heat from the hard slap. "Not until I say so, or you're sleeping in your car tonight. Understand?"

She clenched her teeth, her body trembling again, seething. "I hate you."

"I know."

"Of all the driveways to crash into—"

"That's it—let it out. Let it all out."

"You are *unbelievable.* So full of yourself, and... and you're just..."

"Keep going, Cupcake. You've got more to say—I can tell."

"You're mean, and grumpy, and bossy, and—"

"You know what to say if you want out," I reminded her.

"You're... you're the O.G. Grinch who stole Christmas."

Stifling a laugh, I rubbed her ass, my handprints rising bright against the pale skin. At my soothing touch, a sob of frustration escaped her lips, but no more words about hatred and Grinches.

And most importantly?

No gingerbread. No fucking gingerbread.

She didn't want me to stop.

Maybe there was a fucking Santa Claus after all.

HAWKE

Bringing my lips to her upper thigh once more, I traced a delicate pattern from one side to the other, hands sliding down her outer curves, her scent unraveling me.

"Hawke," she whispered, her voice as shaky as her thighs. She was close. Too close.

"You're ready to come for me now, aren't you, Cupcake?" I whispered.

"Yes! God, yes! Please!"

The desperation in her voice was the sweetest fucking melody.

"Too bad." Getting to my feet, I jerked her hand out of her panties and pinned both of her wrists behind her back. "You need to slow down now, naughty girl. Deep breaths."

She groaned in protest, her chest rising and falling with rapid, shallow breaths as she ignored my command, but hell, it wasn't like I hadn't warned her.

"I said deep breaths, Maddie. Unless you want to break my rules again and deal with another punishment."

Shaking her head, she sucked in a breath, then let it out slowly. Another. Another. I waited patiently, letting her come off the edge a little.

It would make pushing her over the cliff all the sweeter.

I was still holding her wrists captive in one hand, my other hand drifting down to her hip, tugging at the edge of her panties, making her sigh once more.

Touching her was... *fuck*. I still couldn't even believe she was real. Here. Warm and whole and perfect, so damn sweet she made my chest hurt.

As much as I wanted to drag out this delicious punishment, I was growing just as impatient as my girl. Just as desperate.

And the panties—as sexy as they were, decorating her ass like icing—had suddenly become nothing more than the annoying barrier that stood between my mouth and her pussy.

I grabbed my pocket knife, brought the blade to the lace, and sliced through it without another thought, yanking the scrap of fabric from her body and tossing it onto the counter with the knife.

I released her wrists, and she turned to face me.

A faint blush colored her cheeks, a thin sheen of sweat glimmering across her forehead. Her eyes were so blue they nearly stopped my heart.

"What are you staring at?" She smiled, just a little shy. Then she bit her lip, her cheeks darkening even more.

I was in a fucking trance.

"You drive me wild," I whispered, shaking my head. "Absolutely fucking wild."

"So touch me," she said, fisting the front of my hoodie like she might just tear it off if I didn't give her what she wanted. "Please, Hawke. *Please.*"

She was losing her mind, so fucking needy for it, just like me.

Well, hell. I couldn't deny her for one more minute.

Like a heat-seeking missile homing in on its target, I slid my hand between her thighs again.

"More," she whispered, eyelids fluttering closed. "More."

I thrust two fingers deep inside, feeling her body tense, then relax, her hips rocking again, coaxing me into a perfect rhythm.

God, she's so fucking tight. So fucking perfect.

My dick strained against my pants, gunning hard to find out what it felt like to be buried balls deep in that tight, wet heat, letting her milk me for all it was worth, but this wasn't about me right now.

Just her. My naughty little cupcake.

"That's it," I whispered. "Take what you want, Maddie. Fucking take it."

She matched me stroke for stroke, fucking my hand until it was as slick as she was, her body pulsing around me, begging for the release I continued to hold just out of reach.

"Yeah, you're definitely a naughty girl," I teased, slowing my fevered strokes. "But I bet you *damn* sure taste nice."

I slid my fingers out and brought them to my lips, but then changed my mind, moving them to her mouth instead. "Open up, Cupcake."

Maddie parted her wet lips without hesitation, taking my fingers between them. Her tongue was velvet-smooth, and the soft whimpers of pleasure escaping her mouth made my heart thunder once more.

Holy fuck, she's gonna make me come just from sucking on my fingers...

I couldn't take it anymore.

I'd been dreaming about that mouth for hours, enduring the torture of watching her eat, watching her lick her lips, watching her smile, all the while wondering how her kiss would taste, how it would feel, what the fuck it would do to me. I couldn't—*wouldn't* deny myself for another second.

I slid my fingers out of her mouth and into the wild cascade of her hair, and finally—*finally*—I claimed that lush mouth with a fierce kiss.

She sighed into my mouth, hands threading into the back of my hair, the sweet-and-salty flavor of her making me delirious, sending red-hot sparks straight through my chest, straight down to my balls.

Outside, the blizzard raged on, the wind howling mad against the windows, snow and ice determined to bury us, but here in my kitchen in the flickering candle-light, my redhead and I were hot and frantic and alive, her kiss making me dizzy, and *damn*, I could've stayed with her just like that, my hands in her hair, tongue sweeping into her mouth, my arms holding her tight until fucking New Year's if only she'd let me.

But the taste of her divine pussy was all-too-quickly fading from her lips, and more than anything—more than any damn thing I'd ever wanted—I needed another hit.

I pulled back, my lips hot and puffy, her own just as swollen, her chin red from the scratch of my stubble.

I didn't know *what* she saw in my eyes just then, but

hers suddenly widened, staring up at me like a cornered little animal who just realized her fate.

The woman was about to be *utterly* devoured.

13

HAWKE

With a feral grin, I gripped her hips and lifted her up, carrying her to the kitchen table.

"Hawke?" she panted. "Are you—"

"*Hungry.*"

It was the only word I could manage, and it was the fucking truth. I set her down on the table, sliding my hands up her legs and gripping her bare thighs, spreading them.

She was wet and glistening, bare, and as she leaned back on the table, I took a minute to appreciate the view, cataloguing every sexy, beautiful curve as I considered where to put my tongue first.

"So beautiful," I muttered. "So wet." Then, tightening my grip, I pinned her thighs to the table and dipped my head between her legs, inhaling the raw, up-close scent of her.

Another growl vibrated through my chest, making me tremble.

Mine came the call from the wolf.

Mine came the call from the man.

"Mine," I echoed out loud, staking my fucking claim. "*Mine.*"

Heat radiated from her flesh, but I wanted her even hotter. I wanted her on fucking *fire* for me.

"Hands above your head," I said. "Grab the edge of the table and don't let go."

Maddie obeyed at once, and I rewarded her with a gentle kiss on her inner thigh. "Good girl. *So* fucking good."

I pursed my lips and exhaled slowly, blowing a long, lingering breath across her clit that made her thighs quake, her skin erupting in goose bumps. She tried to arch her hips to get closer to my mouth, but I held firm, my powerful hands holding her hostage.

She gritted her teeth, frustration making her blue eyes blaze.

"Guess I'm not the only one who doesn't like being teased," I said. "Too bad you look so fucking good right now, all flustered and worked up for me, wondering what I'll do next. Wondering when I'll finally let you come."

"Hawke," she hissed. "You're so.... so mean."

I laughed, digging my fingers into her thighs. "I told you how things were gonna be tonight, Cupcake. You want out? You know the magic word."

She pressed her lips together and shook her head, stubborn little thing.

"That's what I thought." Still grinning, I blew another hot breath across her clit, making her writhe. Then, without warning, I clamped down on her thighs and pressed my face to that bare pussy, spearing her with my tongue, then dragging it up to swirl over her clit. Maddie cried out in pleasure, but *I* was the one about to fucking lose it.

The taste of her was beyond my wildest fantasies, a rich and heady drug I'd happily overdose on.

I released my hold on her thighs and cupped her ass in both hands, bringing her closer, taking my fill.

Mine. Fucking *mine*.

Maddie clamped her thighs around my head, grinding against my face as I dipped and sucked, kissed and teased, driving myself mad with lust as I pushed her closer and closer to that white-hot edge. I couldn't get enough of her, the feel of her ass in my hands, the taste of her as I slid my tongue inside, fucking her senseless with every stroke.

I felt her getting closer, every muscle in her body tense with anticipation, her skin glowing, her mouth parted in a desperate gasp as she panted and moaned...

Fuck. As much as I enjoyed a good tease, I couldn't back down now. She was too close, too ready to go supernova.

Too fucking beautiful.

I couldn't take it anymore. Suddenly, I *had* to make Maddie come—had to see what she looked like as I sent her right over the fucking cliff.

Sliding two fingers inside her, I sucked her clit, grazing it with my teeth, then flicking it with my tongue as I pumped her deeper, harder, *just* fucking right.

"Hawke!" She squeezed her eyes shut and thrashed on the table like a wild thing. "Oh my God. *Hawke!* Please don't tease me anymore. I can't... I can't hold on. I'm... I'm right there!"

"Then fall," I urged, curling my fingers to hit that perfect spot. "Come for me, Maddie. Let me see you fucking *shatter.*"

I pressed one more deep, soul-shattering kiss to that sweet pussy, moaning against her flesh, and my naughty girl fucking *exploded* for me, hips arching off the table, her body tightening and pulsing around my fingers as the orgasm ravaged her head to toe. I slowed my thrusts as she crested that intense wave, but before she came all the way down, I drew my fingers back and pressed my mouth to her once more, scraping my teeth over her clit, tonguing that pussy until she peaked again and came with another shuddering cry.

Her body finally gave out, and she dropped her hips back down onto the table, totally boneless. I slumped backward and landed in a chair, panting as hard as Maddie. My whole body buzzed.

Fucking hell.

I'd never taken a woman like that, so raw and desperate. And I'd never, ever had a woman run so hot for me, so responsive and eager.

I scrubbed a hand over my mouth, her taste lingering.

I was fucking *intoxicated.*

Bad idea, asshole. Bad, bad idea.

Sweet little Maddie Lockwood was the kind of woman I could get hooked on, real quick. And no matter how good she'd felt, how good she'd tasted, *fuck*...

She was a vice I *really* didn't need.

Time to terminate the situation. I'd given her what she wanted—a nice top-off to a great meal. Now it was time to wish her goodnight, disappear upstairs, and finish myself off in the shower, hoping like hell the storm would break and a tow truck would miraculously appear, hauling her right out of my driveway. Out of my life.

I *had* to say goodbye. Merry fucking Christmas, Cupcake. Happy New Year, have a nice night, have a nice life. That was the smart thing. The *best* thing.

For both of us.

But before I could catch my breath and convince myself to make the damn move, Maddie slid down off the table and—with a devious grin—dropped to her knees in front of me.

14

HAWKE

"M y turn." Still grinning, Maddie ran her hands up my thighs and unfastened my jeans, slipping her hand inside and freeing my cock. "And since you have such a fondness for the color red, *your* safe word is Rudolph. But not just the name—the actual song. You have to sing it in its entirety if you want out."

I blinked at her, lost to the pleasure of her touch as she began to stroke. To squeeze. To...

Oh, fucking *hell*, there wouldn't *be* an out. Not for me.

Even if I *wanted* to sing the song, which—for the record—I damn sure didn't, I wouldn't have been able to.

My cock was in charge now.

Fuck you if you think you're shutting this down, Stevens.

I glanced at my lap. Maddie's fingers looked so small and delicate around me, her eyes wide as she tried to hold on to my ever-stiffening dick.

"Damn," she said softly.

Made me laugh.

"You sure you know what you're doing?" I teased, cupping her face and tracing my thumb across her bottom lip, still puffy from our earlier kiss. "Looks to me like you can barely get your hands around it."

"Hands? Totally overrated." She flashed me another mischievous grin, and then she was on me, the perfect pink "o" of her lips sliding down around the head, tongue stroking me as she took me in inch by torturous inch. Her teeth grazed the sensitive skin—an intense, delicious pain that set my balls on fire.

I shoved my hands into her hair, burying my fingers in it. It was like living fire, the exact color of a Bali sunset, and that shit was fucking *everywhere* now, huge curls that sprung out in all directions. Damn, I loved the feel of those silky locks in my hands almost as much as I loved the feel of her tongue swirling around my tip.

"Fuck, that's... that's so... *good*," I could barely get the words out—girl was making me lose control, siphoning it away from me one red-hot flick of her tongue at a time.

Maddie glanced up at me through her lashes, those adorable freckles dusting her face, her mouth so hot and soft and...

Fuck.

I needed to take it back—all the control she'd stolen, the last thing tethering me to this world. To my humanity. If I didn't, I'd lose myself to the wolf.

Tightening my grip in her hair, I pulled her away, my cock sliding out of her mouth, wet and shining in the candlelight.

"Tap my thigh three times if it's too much," I gritted out, aching to sink back into her mouth. "Got it?"

"We're tapping now?" She smirked, giving me a playful roll of her eyes. "I still remember my safe word, you know."

"Not for long, you won't." I shook my head, the dark, wicked thoughts making my voice hoarse. "Not after what I'm gonna to do to you."

Her eyes widened, but I didn't give her time to ask questions. I guided her head back into my lap, sliding my cock between her lips. Then, with a groan of pleasure I couldn't hold back, I slammed all the way in, so deep I hit the back of her throat.

Maddie gagged, but when I met her eyes again and lifted a brow in question, she moaned softly, her throat relaxing to take me in even deeper.

She feels so fucking amazing...

I bucked my hips and held her head close, fucking that mouth hard and deep as she licked and sucked and moaned, her every movement sending electric shocks throughout my entire fucking body.

"That's it," I whispered, her sucking growing more eager. More insistent. "You're taking it so good for me. *So* fucking good."

God, that fucking mouth. That hair. The freckles, the mischievous glint in her eyes, even as tears streaked down her cheeks from taking me so hard and deep...

And still, she didn't tap out. Didn't do a damn thing but set my entire world on fire.

She moaned again, the sound vibrating across my cock, sending a jolt of pure pleasure straight to my balls. I felt the familiar tingle, the heaviness, the tightness, and knew it was only seconds...

"Maddie, I'm *right* there. I'm... Tap out, Maddie. Fucking tap out!"

She glanced up at me with a devilish gleam in her eyes, hollowing her cheeks once more and sucking me in deep, her tongue undulating, and that was it; game fucking over. I fisted her hair tighter and held her close as I shuddered against her, coming in a furious rush, her throat pulsing as she swallowed it all down.

Girl had the face of a damn Christmas angel, looking up at me with those baby blues as I finally slid out of her mouth, totally spent.

With a soft smile, Maddie rested her cheek against my thigh and sighed, and I stroked her hair, wondering —once again—what the fuck I was doing.

I couldn't pretend to know her innermost secrets, but I *did* know this: as much as she'd loved a good hard spanking, as much as she'd let me eat her pussy on the dinner table and then sucked my dick like a dirty little vixen, Maddie Lockwood was *good*. She was good, she was pure, and she was whole.

And me? I was nothing but a shell, my heart as black as coal. Yeah, I was quick with a smart-ass remark and some dirty pillow talk, and I *damn* sure knew how to put a blush on her cheeks and an ear-to-ear grin on her freckled face But all that stuff was on the outside—what she saw when she looked at me. It was *all* she saw, because that's all I'd dared to show her.

Inside? That shit was a damn war zone, a wasteland I'd never let *anyone* traverse, let alone Maddie. And my wolf? Hell, he was a dark secret I just *couldn't* reveal— not without shattering her entire world. As honest and sincere as she was, everyone had their fucking limits. Seeing the truth of it—of *me*...

No. It would break something inside her I wanted to keep whole, even if I couldn't keep it for myself.

Girls like Maddie—they believed in the fairy tale. They wanted a good man to sweep them off their feet, to give them a whirlwind romance, to treat them like queens. To give them an amazing life.

And why the fuck *shouldn't* they want it? It's exactly what they deserved.

Looking at Maddie now, my perfect little Christmas cupcake, I was pretty sure no one had ever told her the truth—that fairy tales didn't exist. Not in the real world. Just wasn't possible.

For Maddie, *everything* was possible. She probably jumped out of bed every day before the alarm even went off, her face already lit up with that megawatt grin, ready to go out and conquer the world.

Me? I got out of bed every day wondering if today would be the day I'd finally blow my fucking brains out.

Wolf or no wolf—how could I expose her to that shit? How could I risk it, even for one night?

Why had I have even let things go *this* far?

Because you're a selfish prick who destroys everything he touches, and you'll never fucking learn, asshole.

"Hawke? What's wrong?" Maddie glanced up at me with concern in her eyes, scattering my dark thoughts. "Was that... was it okay?"

I forced a smile, rubbing the crease between her eyebrows with the heel of my hand. I didn't want her to feel bad, but my guilt was already seeping in, burning up my insides like battery acid. I couldn't handle this. The soft murmurs. The cuddling. The gazing longingly into each other's eyes and talking about feelings or sharing secrets or whatever the fuck people did after doing what we'd just done.

Some things were better left unsaid. Untouched.

Fuck it.

The wolf inside me reared his head, clawing at my insides, still riled up by her scent. Her presence. He needed out, which meant I needed to shift. To run through the snow and get all this shit out of my system before *I* started wishing for the bullshit fairy tale, too.

"I... I gotta go," I said abruptly, standing up and zipping my pants.

Maddie gaped at me, confusion chasing the concern from her eyes. She looked like she'd been slapped, and not in the sexy way.

Nice move, ace.

"But it's your house," she said. "Where are you going?"

"Dunno," I snapped. "But since it's my house, I can come and go without an interrogation, right?"

I shoved my feet into my boots, not bothering with

the coat. Wouldn't need it anyway—that shit would only get in the way.

At the sound of the door opening, Bella bolted down the stairs and charged right at me.

"Hawke?" Maddie asked again, and the hurt in her voice made me feel like an even bigger douche bag than I was. She was still kneeling half-naked on my kitchen floor, lips swollen and puffy, her hair a tangled mess. Behind me, the kitchen faucet dripped onto the pile of abandoned dishes.

Plunk. Plunk. Plunk.

I couldn't look into her eyes now—it would wreck me. Maybe that's what I deserved, but fuck it, I was taking the easy way out tonight.

"Make yourself at home, Cupcake." I opened the door and stepped out onto the porch, Bella bounding out into the snow ahead of me. "Don't wait up."

Outside, I trudged out behind the garage and out of sight from the windows. Certain she couldn't see me, I stripped out of my clothes and boots, cracked my neck, and let my wolf loose.

With a roar, my muscles elongated, my skin growing thick with fur, bones snapping and popping, ushering in the familiar pain that plowed through me as everything inside shattered and reformed.

Wolf.

I howled into the night, grateful to be out of that human fucking skin.

And then, with Bella at my side, I ran.

So hard, so fast, until everything around me blurred into a raging sea of pure, violent white and I was certain I'd left all that horrible guilt and shame behind.

15

MADDIE

*M*erry Christmas and Happy New Year to you, too, Mr. Grinch.

That was the last straw. Treacherous roads be damned, I would *not* waste another minute of my Christmas vacation with a man who'd rather be alone for the holidays than show one teeny, tiny shred of vulnerability.

The guy had issues—obviously—but screw that. Who didn't? Issues or not, if some good ol' fashioned deep throat at the dinner table wasn't enough to give Hawke Stevens a little ho-ho-holiday cheer, I was all out of ideas.

I blinked away tears that had no business falling and picked myself up off the floor, straightening my ginger-bread shirt, ignoring the bite of cool air on the bare flesh below my waist. There was nothing to be upset about, anyway—it's not like Hawke had left me high and dry, aching for release.

He might've been a dick, but good *lord* he was a full-service dick...

Ugh. Thinking about Hawke's services—and his dick—sent traitorous waves of pleasure coursing through my body again. I'd never felt anything so intense, so hot. My legs were still wobbly, my insides pulsing with aftershocks.

How was that even possible?

Spoiler alert, girl. The man just gave you a full-blown Christmas miracle right there on the kitchen table...

I ran my hands over my ass, still superheated from his touch. I couldn't believe I'd let Hawke spank me like a disobedient child, but there was no denying the truth: I'd loved every second of it. I'd probably be feeling the sting for days.

Jeez, I needed a T-shirt or something to commemorate the occasion. *I ignored the red flags, and all I got was a red ass...*

I shook my head, clearing away the memories of his brutal touch. It didn't matter how good he'd made me feel, how cherished and sexy and strong.

Whatever we'd shared, it was totally temporary, totally casual, and totally over. He'd made that absolutely clear. And just in time, too. I never should've let things get so out of control.

Even if he *could* take me from zero to screaming double orgasm in thirty seconds flat...

Enough. Thoughts of Hawke Stevens end now.

Upstairs, I dressed quickly and got to work gathering up my things. Twenty minutes later, there was still no sign of Hawke, but I was packed and ready to go, dressed in warm layers, my hair and makeup nice and presentable again. I was no longer feeling it with the elf costume, but that didn't mean I had to show up at the Lockwood family Christmas looking like I'd spent the night rolling around on some random mountain man's kitchen table. It was going to be enough of a challenge explaining to my family of perennial worrywarts why I'd decided to drive up here on my own during a snowstorm without telling anyone about my plans—an idea that seemed a lot better in retrospect. Didn't need to add "why do you look like you've just been stuffed like a Christmas turkey?" to their list of questions.

I sighed, telling myself everything would be just fine. The salt trucks had probably been through by now, right? My car was—what had Hawke said? FUBAR?— but maybe I could try the onboard nav again, see if I could finally convince a tow truck to drive up here. Then I'd just wait in the car until the driver arrived.

"You ain't going anywhere tonight. Except inside. With me."

His deep, gravelly voice echoed in my memory, but I dismissed it and dragged my luggage down the stairs. My new plan was solid; with any luck, I'd get to Mom and Dad's rental in time to see the kids before bedtime and gobble up a piece of Mom's homemade chocolate cream pie, all without so much as a backward glance at this cabin *or* the man who owned it.

Too bad your pink bunny vibrator will never live up to that man's tongue...

"Whatever," I said to absolutely no one. "At least Mr. Bunny doesn't throw a tantrum and bail after spending some quality time with me."

Ignoring the heat that swirled in my belly, I layered on my coat and winter gear, stacked my bags into a manageable arrangement, and lugged them outside, closing the door on Hawke Stevens and that very brief, better-left-forgotten chapter of my life.

16

MADDIE

*S*earching *for satellite. Searching for satellite. Searching for satellite...*

After ten minutes, the nav system was no closer to finding the satellite than I was to erasing the white-hot sting of Hawke's touch from my skin.

I clicked off the device and fished through the glove box for the map from the car rental place, hoping I could figure out the right direction toward town.

Hawke lived on the outskirts, but the tiny town center catered to tourists, and it had a bus line as well as private shuttles for the skiers and snowboarders that flooded the area every winter. Assuming I could find my way there, maybe I could catch a shuttle to my parents' place tonight, then have Dad bring me back to Hawke's tomorrow to grab the rest of my stuff from the car and wait for the tow truck.

Not like I'd have to interact with Hawke for that. He wouldn't even need to know we were there.

And if the shuttles weren't running tonight, I could probably find a restaurant or coffee shop to wait out the storm. Some quaint little mountain-view café filled with laughter and clinking glasses and hot cocoa and Christmas music—everything I loved about the holidays but had so often missed out on.

Not this year, though. This year was supposed to be different. I was strong. I was healthy. I'd been given a second chance, and I wasn't about to squander it on a man who couldn't even look me in the eye after I'd sucked him up like a damn Hoover.

I rubbed my fist against my chest, knuckles tracing the now-familiar grooves and ridges of the scar that ran down the front of me like a zipper. It didn't hurt—not anymore. It was a comfort now, a reminder that life was short, that it was meant to be lived with passion and intensity and yes, even a little recklessness. That was the promise I'd made last December, and despite the risks, despite my parents' constant fretting, despite my own deep-seated fears that my doctors' predictions were eventually going to come true, I intended to keep that promise for as long as I could.

A few hours with a sexy, fierce, hot-tempered, seriously messed-up, multiple-orgasm-inducing *recluse* wasn't going to change that. If anything, it only reinforced my desire to keep going. To pick myself up again, dust off my shoulders, charge right back out there, and grab the reindeer by the horns.

To live my life. Truly live it.

I'd taken a colossal risk tonight. I'd done something crazy, something wild, something all for me. And for that, I couldn't be mad—couldn't regret it—no matter how awkwardly and abruptly things had ended.

You've got this, girl.

With renewed hope, I checked the laces on my boots, re-knotted my scarf, and stuffed my hands back into my thick wool mittens. If my map-reading skills were reliable, the town center was a few miles down the mountain—practically a straight shot, save for a couple of forks in the road along the way.

There was a time when a few miles would've felt like an impossible marathon, but not anymore. Now, it was practically a cakewalk.

Passion. Intensity. A little recklessness.

"Let's *do* this thing, bitches."

Leaving most of the luggage in the car, I packed up a few essentials into my shoulder bag, slung it across my chest, and clomped down to the road. Miracle of miracles, it looked like the plows had been through fairly recently, leaving the roads somewhat clear.

Snow was still falling in big, fat gobs, but the wind had eased up, lessening the brutal sting of the cold, and as I set off on my next adventure, I was feeling pretty good about my decision to take matters into my own hands.

The sky was dark, but the snow from the surrounding woods reflected a soft white glow all around me, lighting my path along the road. There was no sound but my breath and the soft crunch of my boots in the snow—the kind of deep, dark silence that didn't exist in New York. The kind that made me feel like the very last person on earth.

It was terrifying and comforting all at once.

After I'd walked a few dozen yards down the road, Hawke's cabin disappeared entirely from view. But that treacherous little body of mine refused to let him go. I was still primed and ready, the fresh panties I'd put on already damp with arousal, my core aching for Hawke's expertly delivered thrusts.

The chemistry between us had been explosive; from the moment he'd opened the door, I'd felt the tension and electricity crackling like a live wire. And once we'd actually touched? Kissed? I was surprised we hadn't burned down the house.

How had things gone from so scorching hot to so completely frigid?

Had I been too forward? I could've sworn he'd wanted me as much as I'd wanted him. Had I misread his signals? Thrown myself at him too easily?

Had I somehow forgotten how to give a decent blow job?

Was that even *possible*?

As the thoughts sped up and collided in my head, I continued my march down the mountain, more determined than ever to put a whole lot of distance between my body and Hawke's filthy mouth.

I felt like I was making good time, but it wasn't too long before the snow-capped evergreens all started to look the same, and without streetlights or passing cars, I couldn't be certain I was still heading in the right direction—if I'd taken all the right forks. After another fifteen minutes of walking, I stopped to catch my breath and get my bearings, and my stomach bottomed out as reality came crashing down.

I had no idea where I was.

Winter's darkness fell hard and fast in the Rockies, and a few dozen yards in the wrong direction could mean a slide down an impossibly steep cliff. A broken neck. Frostbite. Hypothermia. People died out here all the time, just because they'd gotten distracted for a single minute and lost track of their surroundings.

With my thoughts still consumed by Hawke, I didn't even know how long I'd been walking. An hour? Three? Six?

Suddenly, it was as dark as the end of days. The wind was picking up again, my feet soaked through and going numb.

I was—despite my map-reading skills and epic determination to blaze my own trail—utterly, impossibly lost.

And if that wasn't bad enough, I missed him. More than anything, I freaking *missed* him.

Tears froze into two icy tracks down my cheeks.

Oh, Maddie Lockwood, sometimes you are just too stupid to live.

17

HAWKE

Get in there, Bella. Go give our girl a big, wet kiss." I smacked the dog's rump and followed her inside.

Bella and I had done a good hard run, romping together in the snow for the past forty-five minutes, chasing the wind through the ponderosa pines out back. It was cold as balls out there, but hey—nothing like letting my wolf run in the crisp, clean mountain air to clear my fucked-up human head.

The fresh air and exercise made me realize I'd been over-thinking the whole situation. Maddie and I were healthy, consenting adults—no reason we couldn't have a little fun passing the time until the storm broke. She wasn't looking for a damn marriage proposal or the key to all my deep, dark secrets. All that fairy tale crap was in my head, and I'd let it screw with me so badly I'd taken all my bullshit out on her—a thing I'd been trying to avoid since she'd first shown up on my doorstep.

Girl was right—I *was* the O.G. Grinch. But that ended now. For however much time we had left, I'd give that ginger the best goddamn Christmas I could offer.

Starting with stripping her bare and carrying her right up to my bed for a thorough ravishing. It was Christmas Eve, visions of her sweet sugarplum ass were dancing in my head, and it was *long* past time I made her come again.

But first—I owed her an apology. A big one.

Back inside, all the candles had been blown out, the lantern turned off too. The fire in the living room had burned down to embers, and a chill filled the whole damn cabin. Shit just felt... empty.

"Maddie?" I skimmed my fingers across the kitchen table that would now live on in infamy, peering through the darkness for signs of my feisty redhead. "Where you at, Cupcake?"

Nothing.

The tattered lace panties were still on the counter where I'd chucked them, but when I glanced at the hooks on the wall where she'd hung her green scarf and sparkly white hat to dry earlier, I found them empty.

Bella whimpered beside me, and something in my gut twisted into a big-ass knot.

No. No fucking way.

Would she really just bail like that? It was still snowing like a bitch out there. Where the fuck could she possibly go?

No—it made no sense. She *had* to be in the cabin. Upstairs, maybe. After the way I'd acted, it was too much to hope that I'd find her naked and curled up in my bed, eagerly awaiting my return, but maybe she'd passed out in the spare bedroom. I'd told her to make herself at home, after all. Maybe she'd done just that.

"Maddie?" I called out, not caring if I woke her up. "I got something to say to you." With Bella on my heels, I grabbed a flashlight from the kitchen junk drawer and headed upstairs. "Maddie, look. I know I fucked up. I'm sorry. Come on out and let me apologize properly."

No response.

The girl was just... just gone. Her luggage. Her pink bubblegum coat. Her bright red curls. All she'd left behind was a whiff of that sweet vanilla-nutmeg scent, the ruined panties, and—there on the floor just outside the bathroom, dropped in her haste to leave—the small green toiletry bag she'd been so desperate for me to fetch.

For some fucked-up reason I did *not* want to admit, the sight of it made my heart hurt.

"What'll you do without your special conditioner, Cupcake?" I scooped it up and yanked open the zipper, wondering just what was so special about it, anyway.

But what I found inside wasn't conditioner at all. It was a whole mess of prescription bottles, each one printed with her name and precise directions. *Take twice daily with water. Take once daily before bed. Do not take on an empty stomach.* I didn't recognize the names of the drugs, but I was pretty damn sure they weren't just for the low blood sugar thing she'd mentioned.

What the hell?

Her rental car was still D.O.A. at the bottom of the driveway, and Bella and I hadn't seen or heard any other cars or a tow truck pull up; even out back in the woods, one of us would've sensed something.

Which meant Maddie had likely taken off on foot.

And she'd forgotten her damn meds.

Worry kicked into overdrive.

Fucking hell. One stupid argument, and now I was in for a search-and-rescue.

Bella barked at me, eyeing me up from the hallway like, *What are you gonna do now, you stupid prick?*

Right. Like I had all the fucking answers.

I used to think so—used to think I knew it all. I'd

been all over the globe, had seen the best and worst humanity had to offer. I'd even survived this fucked-up mutant bullshit military experiment and, as far as I could tell, still had a lot of years left in me, assuming I didn't cash in my chips first.

But in the handful of hours since that crazy girl had crash-landed in my driveway, I was starting to realize I didn't know *jack* about *shit* about *squat*.

I sighed and palmed Bella's head. "Hold the fort down for me, Bells. I gotta go track down that pain-in-the-ass redhead and drag her back here for another good spanking."

HAWKE

Tracking Maddie wouldn't be hard—security cam footage confirmed she'd stashed her luggage in the car not long after I'd left the cabin, then hit the road on foot about ten minutes later, heading toward town.

And tracking people down? Hell, my wolf was practically *made* for that shit.

Problem was—after everything I'd put her through tonight—Maddie damn sure didn't need to see me wolf out. Girl probably had no idea supernaturals even existed, despite the fact that she lived in the same city where the royal vampire family ruled the roost and—last I'd heard—spent most of their nights battling for dominance in an endless circle-jerk with the city's various demonic crime syndicates. Every last one of those fanged and furred fuckers—and yeah, I counted myself among them—came with a whole mess of darkness and violence humans were much better off not knowing about.

Especially sweet, innocent humans like Maddie.

But as much as I'd love to sidestep an existential crisis over the whole monsters-are-real revelation, I couldn't. Time was the enemy in an exposure scenario like this. Maddie didn't have the proper winter gear, and at this altitude, with a below-zero wind chill, even twenty minutes out in the elements could lead to severe hypothermia—and that wasn't even taking into account her medical situation.

I was fucking clueless.

I must be a real bastard for her to risk freezing to death just to get away from me...

Fresh guilt gnawed at my chest, but that burn was no less than I deserved.

Without another thought, I stripped out of my clothes and headed back out, shifting the instant my feet hit the snow.

The familiar pain tore through my body as I changed from man to wolf and finally set off, following her footprints and her sweet, warm scent.

Usually when I shifted, I let the wolf take over completely, his animalistic thoughts and instincts taking charge while I checked out of my human mind, grateful for the break. But tonight, I needed both.

The wolf could track her, but it was the man who'd have to bring her back. Who'd have to try not to scare the fuck out of her. Who'd have to make her understand that the world was filled with more nightmares than she'd ever imagined.

And, as hard as it was to admit, it was the man who'd have to fucking apologize for treating her like shit—and hope like hell she could find it in her heart to forgive me.

I loped down the dark road, careful not to lose her trail. The wind was a real menace now, whipping through my fur and making it hard to see. Hard to fucking concentrate.

There wasn't a single vehicle on the road, the night so dark and stormy I felt like I was trapped inside a snow globe. Every time the snow let up for one lousy second, someone picked up the world and gave it another good, hard shake, blinding me once again.

Fifteen minutes on, and *fuck*, still no sign of her. Just the footprints that were quickly filling with fresh snow. Even her scent was beginning to fade.

I followed the half-buried trail down the main road until the footprints forked onto a service road that led into Rocky Mountain National Park.

If I could've cursed into the wind just then, I fucking would have. Instead, all I could do was howl.

My heart slammed inside my chest, desperation making the wolf as antsy as it made the man. Bad news. *Real* fucking bad. The snow was deeper here than on the main road, and a mile or two in, she'd end up in the back country.

Or worse.

Eight thousand feet up, there were plenty of places to fall off the edge of the earth, never to be heard from again.

Come on, Cupcake. Where the fuck are you?

I plodded through the snow, scanning ahead for a flash of color against the blinding white backdrop—that ridiculous bubblegum coat, the green scarf, a lock of flame-red hair, *anything...*

I was about to bolt back home and call the *real* search-and-rescue, call in every last favor I had just to get a chopper up here and some boots on the ground. But that plan was already a no-go; the phones were still down, and my sat-phone had crapped out months ago.

Nope. This was on me. I *had* to fucking find her—no room for failure on this one.

I continued on, following her trail through the thick blanket of snow. No one else had been through here, and the footprints were relatively fresh, which meant she couldn't have gotten too far...

The wind shifted, carrying the scent of something sweet and familiar to my senses. Vanilla. Fucking vanilla and nutmeg and the first shred of hope I'd felt in an hour.

I charged ahead, and there, like a fucking miracle, I saw it. Something bright pink and puffy shuffling through the trees about thirty yards ahead.

I broke into a run. Poor girl was dragging ass, barely lifting her feet, every step a challenge. Then, finally, she stopped. Just stopped and looked up at the sky like she was five seconds from giving up.

Another few minutes of this shit, and she'd probably just fall over and freeze to death.

Or worse, I realized with a jolt.

Maddie was no more than ten feet away from a sheer drop-off. The boundary was normally well-marked, but this area of the park was closed for the winter and all the trails were hidden by the snow. She'd wandered too far off the path, and she had no idea how close to death she truly was.

Fuck. There was no time for subtlety. No time to plan a graceful transition and calm explanation. No time to do anything but charge right for her.

I shot through the snow, not stopping until I was

right in front of her, blocking her path to the deadly drop-off.

Maddie lowered her gaze from the sky. The instant she saw me, she froze.

"Oh no," she gasped, so faint it was little more than a whisper of frozen white breath on the air.

The scent of her fear washed over me like a tidal wave.

But the sight of her tear-streaked face? That shit damn near gutted me.

Whether it was from sheer terror or the frigid temperatures or both, Maddie was shivering from head to toe, her cheeks bright pink, her nose running, her lips as pale as death.

She was in trouble. Serious fucking trouble. And in that moment, impossible and crazy as it sounded, I knew without a doubt that Maddie Lockwood had become a hell of a lot more to me than a warm place to bury my dick on Christmas Eve.

I let out a low, warning growl, slowly loping closer, nudging her back toward the service road and away from the drop-off. She took a step backward, then another, but she was scared and cold and uncoordinated, and the next step sent her stumbling to her knees.

I waited for her to get up. To run. To bolt for the

cabin, where I could shift and sneak in through the back door, meeting her just in time.

But Maddie didn't move.

Fuck. Don't give up on me now, Cupcake. Don't you fucking give up.

I approached her slowly, nudging her hand with my muzzle, trying not to scare the shit out of her. But judging from her scent, I knew it couldn't be helped.

She didn't move, staring at me as intently as I stared at her, the world falling silent around us.

Her blue eyes were wide with wonder.

"You're... you're so beautiful," she whispered, then laughed. The woman actually laughed. When she spoke again, her voice was soft, but sure. "Maybe you're planning to eat me, but I just had to tell you that. As for my last words... Well, I've had a pretty good run, Mr. Wolf. Maybe not as long as I'd hoped, but a heck of a lot longer than anyone thought possible, and that's saying something, isn't it? And tonight wasn't so bad, as far as last nights go. A good meal, a couple of top-notch orgasms..." She laughed again, shaking her head. "And now I'm sitting here talking to a wolf who's probably two seconds from tearing out my throat, but hey. There are worse Christmas tragedies, right? Burning yourself to a crisp trying to deep-fry a turkey indoors, for instance. Or falling and breaking your neck trying to slide down a chimney in a Santa suit. Death by wolf-mauling on the side of a mountain feels much more badass, so thanks for that."

Another soft smile, the tears still leaking from her eyes, and then the crazy girl slid off her mitten and held out her hand.

I don't know what the fuck came over me, but I couldn't help myself. I licked her palm, then nuzzled into her touch, letting her stroke the fur behind my ears, just like she'd done to Bella earlier.

Even in my wolf form, her touch felt incredible.

"You're a good boy, Mr. Wolf," she said. "Maybe you won't eat me after all. Or maybe I'm hallucinating, or possibly already dead. That seems like the most likely scenario, doesn't it?"

She lowered her hand, sadness creeping back into her face.

No. No. *Fuck* that.

In a flash, I reared up on my hind legs and shifted.

Then, standing naked before her, I held out my hand and said, "You're wrong about that, Cupcake. I'm *definitely* going to eat you. But not until I get you home."

HAWKE

Ignoring my outstretched hand, Maddie screamed and scrambled to her feet, and this time, I didn't need to scent her fear to know she was fucking terrified.

She'd just witnessed a wolf transform into a man before her eyes.

A man who now stood in the middle of a snowstorm, buck naked, hoping like hell I could convince her I was real and not some exposure-induced hallucination.

"Hey," I said gently, holding up my hands in surrender. "I know this looks balls-out crazy, and I know you've got a million questions. I will answer *all* of them, Maddie. I swear it. But this is real. I'm a wolf shifter, and I'm here, and I *promise* it's gonna be alright—I fucking promise you. But I need to get you out of the elements before you go hypothermic."

Maddie didn't respond. Just continued to gape, her hand pressed to her heart, breath rushing out in thick white puffs.

"Talk to me, Maddie. I need to know *exactly* what you're feeling right now." I grabbed her upper arms. She flinched, but I didn't let go. "Any numbness? Dizziness? Blurred vision?"

She finally opened her mouth to speak, but she was shivering so hard she could barely get the words out. "You... you're... you're Mr. Wolf?"

"Answer me, Maddie. Can you feel your toes?"

"I... yes." She closed her eyes, another shudder wracking her body. When she looked at me again, some of the shock and confusion had cleared, but she was still wary. "I'm... cold. And you... you're a *wolf* shifter? But... what? How?"

"Long story, and I'll tell you the whole thing. Back home. In front of a fire. With a stiff drink for me and something hot for you. Deal?"

"But you... you're a... a wolf?" she said again. "And you're..." Her eyes widened. "Oh my god, Hawke. You're naked!" she exclaimed, as if she'd only just now realized it. "Here—take this!"

She hastily handed over her mitten, and I couldn't help it—I fucking cracked up, relief more than humor unleashing the laughter inside me.

I dangled the snow-crusted mitten between us. "And I'm supposed to put this *where*, exactly?"

"Hawke!" she gasped. "You could die out here like that! Or... catch a cold in your... I don't know. It's dangerous!"

"No, cupcake. I'm fine—trust me. Shifters are built differently. I can feel the cold, but it doesn't effect me the same way. Not as a wolf and not as a man. I'm more worried about you right now."

"I'm... I'm okay. Just... embarrassed? Relieved?" She pressed a hand to her forehead, her eyes clearing. "God, that was stupid. I never should've left your place."

"You got that right." I grabbed her arms again, looking her over more closely. She seemed okay. Trembling from the cold, probably uncomfortable as hell, but not confused or uncoordinated, especially given the fact I'd just shifted in front of her. I couldn't tell what condition her toes were in, but she didn't appear to be hypothermic. "You scared the shit out of me, Maddie."

"Yeah?" Maddie tried to pull away, but I wasn't letting her go. Not this time. "Well you... you pissed me off."

Feeling better, I see.

The wind buffeted my back, shaking loose a pile of snow from the canopy of ponderosas overhead, dusting us both in fresh snow.

But Maddie was undeterred.

"I don't know what your problem is, Mr. Wolf," she said, glowering at me, "but you need to get your shit together. Seriously."

That anger must've been fueling her pretty good, because the color had returned to her lips, and now she struggled against me in earnest, pushing on my chest, desperately trying to pry herself out of my grip.

Too damn bad. I had her now. I wasn't letting her out of my sight.

"*I* need to get my shit together?" I bit back a bitter laugh. "I'm not the one who nearly walked myself off the edge of the earth in the middle of a blizzard. So forgive me if I don't agree with your keen analysis of the situation, Cupcake, but you ain't exactly thinking straight, either. And by the way, next time you decide to take a stroll through Rocky Mountain National Park during a snowstorm, you might want to bring your meds."

Her eyes blazed with fresh anger. "You... you went through my *things*?"

"Sorry, Cupcake. You bailed. Technically, they're my things now."

She shook her head, skewering me with a look that would've shriveled my balls if the wind chill hadn't beaten her to it. "You are the very *definition* of a bad idea. I never should've—"

"Never should've *what*, Cupcake?" I leaned in close, so close I could count her fucking freckles. "Never should've crashed into my driveway? Knocked on my door? Hiked halfway down this mountain in a crazy-ass storm with no gear?" I dipped my head, my mouth so close to hers we were sharing the same white breath. "Or are you talking about the part where you spread your legs and offered up that pussy like an all-you-can-eat Christmas buffet?"

Maddie shoved me so hard I nearly stumbled backward, but I held her in a vice grip anyway, righting myself before we both fell.

"You are such an *asshole!*" She banged her fists against my chest, one bare, the other still mittened, fresh tears brimming in her eyes. "What in god's name made you so mean? Because wolf or not, you've got heartless bastard down to an art form, Hawke. And trust me, no one is born that way."

"Yeah, you got me there, Cupcake. I wasn't born this way at all. The world took its sweet-ass time carving out *my* heart."

"That's not an answer," she said.

I scoffed. "Tough shit. It's the only one you're gonna get."

"What happened to you?"

I opened my mouth and took a deep breath of icy

cold air, so close to telling her to fuck off. To saying something so cruel and cold, it would give new meaning to the phrase "heartless bastard"—something that would shut her up until the storm passed and I could finally get her the fuck out of my life for good.

But then out of nowhere she slid her bare hand against my cheek, smoothing her thumb across my lips, her big blue eyes full of something so fucking rare and beautiful, it made my chest ache. I couldn't even give it a name.

One touch, one look, and sweet little Maddie Lockwood had completely diffused me.

Again.

I kissed her palm, closing my eyes and inhaling the scent of her skin. When I finally found the words to respond, my voice was a scratchy whisper, and I couldn't bring myself to meet her eyes again, so damn afraid that I'd fall right into them, lost forever. "There are things in this world, Maddie... things I'd give my life to keep you safe from."

"Like the fact that wolf shifters are real?"

I nodded. "Among other things."

"Other things." She blew out a breath and nodded, and I braced myself for a barrage of questions, but they didn't come. Maddie didn't push. Didn't pry. Just stretched up on her toes and leaned into me, brushing her cool lips against my cheek, whispering words that cut me deep in the best possible way. "Thank you for finding me. I missed you, Hawke."

"Missed you too, Cupcake. More than you fucking know."

I finally found the courage to meet her eyes again, and when I did, my girl grinned up at me, and for the briefest instant I was pretty damn sure I finally understood the true meaning of Christmas.

But as quickly as it'd appeared, her smile fell away, the color leeching once more from her face. She swayed against me, all out of fight, all out of steam.

She didn't argue when I scooped her up into my arms and held her against my chest. Her whole body trembled with cold and exhaustion, and I could feel her heart slamming against her rib cage, right through my bare chest, right down to my bones.

I wanted to kill her for being so stubborn and stupid, for putting her precious life at risk just because I'd pulled a dick move back at the cabin.

But more than that, I just wanted to hold her close. To keep her safe. To take care of her.

To give her everything she fucking deserved.

And that feeling—the feeling of being responsible for another human being, and *wanting* that responsibility, *welcoming* it—scared the ever-loving *shit* out of me.

But I was done running from it. Done running from *her*.

"Hang in there, Cupcake." I pressed a kiss to her ice-cold forehead, tightened my hold on her, and started the trek back to the cabin. "I'm taking you home."

HAWKE

S hifters," she breathed. "Vampires. Fae. Demons. Witches. All of them are real?"

"Yeah, Maddie. They're real. You know what else is real? Hypothermia. You could've... you could've fucking *died* out there tonight. Don't you get that?"

I shoved my hands through my hair and paced the living room, absolutely fucking *beside* myself as Maddie sat shivering on the couch.

The moment we'd returned to the cabin, I'd put all her questions on pause and ordered her into a steaming hot shower while I fetched her luggage from the car— again. When she finally returned to the living room dressed in another Christmas getup—PJs this time, her tops and bottoms covered in little snowmen—I wrapped her in a blanket, dragged the couch right up close to the fireplace, and spoon-fed her half a can of chicken noodle soup I'd warmed up with the camping stove.

Bella was in on the recovery efforts, too, refusing to leave Maddie's side, keeping watch outside the bathroom door while she'd showered and dressed, sticking to her like a shadow every time she moved. Now, the dog was practically sitting in Maddie's lap on the couch.

I tried to relax. Tried to fucking breathe. Maddie was safe now. Back under my roof. Under my care.

But my girl was still pale. Still trembling.

I wanted to throttle her.

And then I wanted to kiss her.

The thought of losing her—the thought of anything bad happening to her... *Fuck.* It'd done something irreparable, cracked open a part of me I'd long thought buried. It was more ferocious than my wolf, more intense, more... everything. And now that it'd been unleashed, I couldn't lock it down again.

I didn't want to.

"Look, I get it," I said. "I shouldn't even exist. It's insane—the stuff of nightmares and B-movies. I know it's a shock to you, and I meant what I said out there—I *will* answer your questions. Every last one. But fuck, Maddie. I've got questions too. And I think I've earned some answers—starting with why the hell you took off into the wilderness in the middle of a treacherous storm without your meds."

I couldn't bring myself to ask why she even *needed* those pills in the first place, but that question was tearing me up inside, too. Was she sick?

Was she... was she fucking *dying*?

"That part was an accident," she said softly, lowering her eyes. "I didn't mean to leave them behind."

"But you *damn* sure meant to leave the safety of this cabin, right? Packed up all your shit, dragged your ass out to the middle of the park in white-out conditions, no gear, no working phone, not even a headlamp. No way to signal for help if you got in over your head, which— newsflash, Cupcake—you did. You fucking did."

"I'm *fine*, Hawke," she insisted, despite the fact that her teeth were still chattering. "The fire's helping. *You're* helping. You and Bella both. Wait—scratch that. It's actually three of you now. The wolf... We're counting him, too, right? I mean... it is a *him*, isn't it? Or can you have a female wolf if your human body is male?"

"The wolf is definitely a he," I said, unable to keep the smile from my lips. She was too fucking adorable, even when she was driving me crazy. "The wolf is still me, Maddie. Just... just a different version of me. That's probably the easiest way to think of it."

"Easy for you, maybe. Personally? My head's about

to explode." She smiled, then nuzzled Bella's face. "You're just a dog, though, right Bells? A very good, very pretty dog who deserves all the belly rubs and doggy treats in the world, yes you do. Yes, you surely do."

Bella wagged her tail, yelping and hopping around on the couch like she'd just found her fucking soulmate.

While Maddie and Bella continued with their love-fest, one step away from braiding each other's hair and exchanging Best Friends Forever charms, I tossed another log onto the fire and stoked the flames, trying to warm things up for Maddie. The power was still out, and this was our only heat source.

"Hawke, does Bella know you're... you know. *You*?"

"A wolf, you mean? Yeah, she knows." I reached over and rubbed one of Bella's ears. "She saw me shift on our very first date, didn't you, girl?"

I told Maddie the story of how I'd found the dog abandoned in the woods, wounded and emaciated. How my wolf had chased off the mountain lion that had nearly eaten the poor girl.

"Ever since then," I said, "we've been inseparable."

"She doesn't get freaked out about it? Like when you shift back and forth or do... whatever wolf things you do out there?"

"Nah. Animals are different. They can sense things humans can't. She knows I've got her back, and that's all that counts." I sat down on the couch, shooing Bella away. Dog didn't go far—just curled up on the floor in front of Maddie's feet, still keeping a close watch over her new pal.

"So much for having her back," Maddie teased. When I didn't return her laugh, she gazed off into the flames and sighed. "You're pissed—I can feel it. Well, that's okay. I'm still pissed at you, too, for the record. It's just that the whole saving-my-life-thing is kind of outweighing the you-being-a-jerk thing at the moment."

"I'm not pissed, Maddie. I'm just..." I groaned, then grabbed her hand, holding it tight. "What if I hadn't come after you tonight?"

She shrugged. "But you *did* come."

"That's not the point."

"Uh-oh. Now I *know* you're pissed. I set you up for the perfect sex joke, and you didn't even—"

"*Maddie.*"

With a heavy sigh, she stretched out her legs, wiggling her toes before the fire. "Honestly? I don't know. I was upset with how you left things after dinner, and missing my family, and feeling like the biggest failure ever, and I just... I guess I just felt the walls closing in on me. I wanted out. So, out I went. My mom says I have impulse control issues. Once I get an urge to do something, I go for it, consequences be damned."

"I get it, Cupcake. I do. Hell, *impulse control issues* is practically my middle name. But what you did tonight? That was *beyond* impulsive. That was reckless and stupid and the exact kind of shit that earns people a one-way ticket to the E.R.—and that's if they're *lucky*. You walk that line enough times, one day you'll end up on the wrong side of it, no way back."

"Or maybe your life starts out on the wrong side to begin with, and walking that line is your only way out." Maddie glanced over at me again, her eyes glazed with tears. "You know what, Hawke? I spent way too many years feeling like all I could do was peek out through the window and watch life pass me by. I was trapped. Literally trapped. I was technically alive, sure, but I wasn't *living*. It felt like a death sentence." A tear slipped down her cheek, and she dashed it away, a smile rising on her face. "But last Christmas, I got a second chance, and I made myself a promise: Not another *minute* stuck on the inside looking out. Only living—truly living, with all the risks that come with it. Even the reckless ones. *Especially* those."

She held my gaze, and I waited for her to fill in the blanks. To explain that second chance. I suspected it had something to do with all the meds, but I still couldn't bring myself to ask.

Instead, I moved down to the other end of the couch

and took her feet into my lap, working them over one at a time, pressing my thumbs into her arches until I finally felt her relax.

The fire crackled and popped, and a comfortable silence drifted between us, Bella and Maddie both sighing contentedly.

Home.

The word jumped into my head without warning. But before I could even *think* about denying it, Bella finally trotted off upstairs in search of something more interesting, and the moment passed.

Maddie scooted closer, draping her legs over my lap, her ass right up against my thigh.

"As much as I appreciate your efforts to distract me," she said with another smile, "I still have a lot of questions."

"Yeah, I kinda figured."

"First, we need to get the big one out of the way." She took a deep breath, then said, "Why the heck did you make fun of me for naming my dog Turkey when you're a wolf named Hawke?"

"That's your big opener, huh?" I cracked up. "Fine. I got the name when I was born, long before I became a wolf. Turkey wasn't so lucky, the poor bastard."

Maddie returned my laughter, but it faded quickly,

her face turning serious, and I knew what was coming next.

"How did it happen?" she whispered. "Did you get bitten, or..."

"I'll tell you, Maddie. But it's not a pleasant story." I reached up and cupped her face, smoothing my thumb over her cheek.

"You can tell me anything, Hawke. Anything at all." Her eyes were so earnest, so sincere. "I'm not going anywhere. I promise."

I nodded and leaned in close, brushing a soft kiss to her lips.

And then, before I knew it, the whole damn story was spilling out of me.

HAWKE

As the fire crackled before us, I told Maddie about the tragic deaths of my mom and sister, the military enlistment, the move into the black-ops shit—the darkest fucking days of my life.

I told her about all the dirty missions in the world's most fucked-up places, how I still had nightmares about them. Could still hear men screaming and begging for death—men from both sides of the line.

And then, I told her about the experiments. The military's endless quest to build a better, stronger, unstoppable army.

"I still don't understand the science behind it," I said. "Something about DNA and genetic sequencing and molecular reprogramming... The experiments weren't exactly optional or consensual, so they didn't bother explaining it.

But one night, we started getting injections, and then, in a matter of weeks, soldiers were just... just fucking shifting in the field. Uncontrolled, untrained, not knowing what the fuck was happening to us. It was terrifying, Maddie. More terrifying than all the enemies we'd ever faced. Because at least with them, we knew who our targets were. Knew how to take them out. This was... this was just madness."

"It's a lot harder to fight the enemy when the enemy is your own body," she said softly, dashing away another tear. "God, Hawke. I can't believe they put you through that. I'm so sorry."

"Not gonna lie—it fucking sucked. But that was years ago. I've had a decade to accept it. To learn how to control the shifts. Now, the wolf is just another version of me, like I said. At this point? Fucked up as it sounds, I can't imagine *not* having him with me."

"Is that how all shifters are made, then? In labs?"

"No, not at all. Most are true supernaturals. They're purebreds born into a family line of shifters. Not just wolves, either. Bears, lions, panthers, birds of prey... all sorts of animals."

"But if that's true, and the military wanted shifters, why not just recruit *actual* shifters? Surely some of the military brass know about their existence, right?"

"Sure, but there aren't enough of them, especially in

the States. Purebred shifters are a dying breed. And supernaturals don't like to fight human wars—it would put them on the radar, and if there's one thing all the different supernatural factions agree on, it's that exposure to humans is bad for *everyone*."

"Yeah, I guess that makes sense. Humans would freak out if they knew. I'm freaking out, to tell you the truth."

"Freaking out is one thing. Going on vigilante killing sprees, most likely getting themselves killed in the process? That's a whole 'nother ball of bullshit." I shook my head, imagining some of the half-cocked hunters I'd seen up in these parts trying to go after shifters and vamps instead of rabbits and deer. "Anyway, the military wasn't actually trying to create shifters—not in the strict sense of the word. They just wanted to enhance human soldiers with what they thought were the best, most useful traits from the animal community. The pack mentality, the ability to hunt and track prey, heightened survival instincts, speed and strength, power, stuff like that."

"But something went wrong in Dr. Frankenstein's lab, I take it."

"Exactly. The experiments were unprecedented—no data to rely on, no techniques to replicate. We were the first human test subjects. They had no way to predict the outcomes."

"How many of you are there? The lab-created shifters, I mean."

"In the world? I have no idea—it's all highly classi-fied, highly compartmentalized by design. They don't want us finding out about each other or blowing the lid off their experiments. But in my unit, there were a dozen of us. Two died immediately after the first injection. Two more died during their first shifts—their bodies couldn't handle it. Just... just gave out." I swallowed the knot of grief in my throat. "Three died in combat. Despite our enhanced strength and healing abilities, we're not immortal. We still go down for a well-aimed bullet, same as a regular Joe."

"So there are only five of you from the unit left?"

"Far as I know, yeah."

"You don't keep in touch?"

"It's not like there's a Facebook group for the mili-tary's lab rats, Maddie. Besides, the shit we saw out there... the things we had to do to survive... Sometimes I think we avoid each other because we just don't want to be reminded of..." I trailed off as a shiver crawled down my spine, all the old ghosts stopping by to say hello. "Anyway, that's all in the past. This is my life now, and I've accepted it. Those men will always be my brothers

—I don't need to keep in touch to know that. To feel it. I just... I don't want to go back."

Maddie nodded. "I understand about not wanting to go back."

In that moment, her eyes were so blue, so bright, she looked again like an angel. I reached up and tugged on one of her curls, wrapping it around my finger, memorizing the silky feel of it. The curls, the blue eyes, her soft smile... all of it anchored me to the present. To her. To the warmth spreading through my chest.

"Do you know any natural-born shifters?" she asked. "Have you ever seen any?"

"They're around, sure. Got a few packs here in Colorado, actually, but they're pretty exclusive. Stick to their own kind, try to keep a low profile, don't exactly put out the welcome mat for strangers. I had a few beers with one guy a while back, though—shifter named Cole Diamante, passing through from upstate New York. Real good guy, too. Bit of a recluse, like me. Lone wolf, no pack, though I hear he's in pretty deep with the Redthorne vampires now. Crazy, if you ask me. Even if I was a purebred... Nope. Ain't enough cash in the world to get *me* into bed with any ruling supers, especially the royals. Dorian Redthorne can be a brutal motherfucker when he has to be, and—"

"Wait. *Dorian* Redthorne?" Her eyes widened, her body going rigid beside me. "CEO of FierceConnect?"

I wasn't surprised that she'd heard of him, especially in her line of work. FierceConnect was a well-known social gaming company headquartered in New York. "The one and only."

She pressed a hand to her chest. "He's... he's a *vampire*?"

"A vampire?" I laughed. "He's the vampire *king*, Maddie. Top of the supernatural food chain. Arguably the most powerful supernatural in the world."

"He's my client! He and his partner Aiden Donavon —I work on some of FierceConnect's web and social media stuff, and... Oh, no. Don't tell me Aiden's a vampire, too."

"Along with most of the staff, from what I understand."

"But that's... that's crazy! I feel like that's something they should disclose in the contract!"

I shook my head. "Exposure, remember? It's not just dangerous for supernaturals, but for humans, too. Most people are better off not knowing about our existence. The ones who do know about us either learn to keep their mouths shut, or—"

"Or what?" Her hand moved up to her throat. "Dorian Redthorne tears out their jugulars?"

"Actually, I'm pretty sure the youngest brother's the *real* violent one. Gabriel—quite the reputation, that guy. But no, they don't make a habit of killing humans. The trouble usually comes from *other* humans. People start talking about monsters being real, and everyone around them assumes they're crazy."

"With good reason," she said, her voice fading into a whisper. "This *is* crazy. All of it."

"Doesn't make it any less real."

After a long beat, she glanced up at me and smiled, letting out a long, slow breath. "I'm... I'm glad it's real. Glad *you're* real."

"Yeah? Well, I'm glad you're real, too, Cupcake."

Her cheeks darkened, and *damn* if I didn't want to spend my whole life making her blush like that.

"Can I ask you something?" I took her face in my hands again, gazing into those beautiful eyes. "When you first saw me out there—the wolf, I mean... I knew you were scared. I could scent your fear. But you didn't run. Didn't fight. Didn't even freak out. Why?"

She closed her eyes and shook her head. "It's silly. You'll make fun of me if I tell you."

"I promise I won't. Not this time."

She opened her eyes again, her breath warm and sweet against my lips. "I was lost out there, Hawke. Freezing my ass off. Kicking myself for being so stupid,

But then, just before you showed up, there was a break in the clouds, and I looked up through the pines and saw the North star. It felt like a sign, you know? Like a true Christmas miracle. So I made a wish on it, and when I turned around, there you were. Sure, I was scared. I mean, hello. Wolf. But I knew—I believed—that whatever would happen next was meant to be. That it was all part of my wish, for better or worse."

I couldn't help my grin. "You wished for a wolf?"

"No." She smiled at me, her eyes shining with emotion. With happiness. With wonder. Then, tracing her thumb along my jaw, she whispered, "I wished for one more second chance."

HAWKE

Maddie curled into my embrace, a comfortable silence settling in as she tried to process everything I'd just told her.

It was a lot for her to digest, and all things considered, she was hanging in there pretty well.

Holding her close, I stroked her hair, and she moaned softly.

Damn, she was always so responsive to my touch. Even now, after everything.

I didn't want to stop. I *wouldn't* stop; whatever time we had left, I'd spend it with my hands on her. Naked, clothed, covered in gingerbread cookies or snowmen, I didn't care. As long as I didn't have to let her go.

But despite our physical closeness, something still sat between us—a chilly distance that I needed to close.

Now.

I sucked in a deep breath, then let it out, steadying myself. After everything I'd confessed tonight, this one —this final thing—felt damn near insurmountable. But I had to get it out. I owed her that.

"Maddie, listen," I said, tightening my hold on her. "About before... I know it's my fault that you left. I didn't mean to make you feel bad. You know that, right?"

She didn't answer. Just peered up at me, watching. Waiting. Refusing to make it easy on me, which was something I'd come to expect from my fiery little Cupcake.

"I got too far into my head," I continued. "Totally freaked myself out and took it all out on you. It wasn't fair. It was downright shitty, and I'm sorry. Truly sorry."

Not a word.

"I was a dick."

Nothing.

"A total asshole."

Still nothing.

"A dick wrapped up in an asshole, tied up in a big red Christmas bow, with dicks and assholes stamped all over it."

She bit back a smile at that, her eyes dancing with amusement. It felt like a victory, and it took everything I had not to whoop with joy and relief.

"Hmm," she said, sitting up so she could glare at me a little harder. "When you say you're sorry, do you mean for making fun of my elf costume?"

"No, I—"

"Or for calling me an idiot for driving in this weather?"

"Maddie, it's—"

"Or for snapping at me for wanting hot chocolate, even though that's a perfectly reasonable holiday request, and a simple 'Sorry, I don't have any' would've sufficed?"

"I said I was—"

"Or how about for sawing off my underwear and leaving me on the floor after you did all those... all those *things* to me?" Her smile faded away, her eyes full of new fire, a new blush staining her neck and cheeks.

Guess we found your kryptonite, too, Cupcake.

"*Did* all those things to you?" I asked, my voice turning dangerously low, my dick stirring at the memory of her lips, her tongue, her soft curls in my hands as I'd fucked that smart little mouth. "I know I'm a first-rate asshole—and you're just hitting the tip of the iceberg with that list of yours, believe me. But don't you *dare* suggest you didn't want those things. You were drenched for me, Maddie. You were red hot." I traced my thumb across her lips, making her shiver. "And you could've ended it at any time."

Maddie rolled her eyes and forced out a dismissive laugh, but I saw right through it.

I slid a hand down and wrapped it around her thigh, making her squirm. "In fact, if I were a bettin' man, I'd wager you're thinking about those things again right now, wondering when—not *if*, but *when*—I'm gonna do them to you again."

"Too bad," she muttered, voice quavering. "You... You'd lose that bet."

"Doubt it." I pushed her backward onto the couch and climbed on top of her, pinning her wrists above her head. Her eyes widened, her breasts swelling against my chest. That soft, sensual mouth parted—half in question, half in desire—and I brushed my lips across it, making her breath catch.

With a trail of light kisses, I dragged my mouth to her ear.

"Thing is, Cupcake, I *am* going to do those things to you again," I whispered, my dick growing hard as she trembled beneath me. "Maybe right now." I kissed her neck. "Maybe in an hour." Her jaw. "Or maybe later, after you fall asleep in my bed without these adorable little snowman pajamas, because yes, I'll be removing those too." I brought my lips to her ear again, barely able to control my own ragged breathing, my thundering heart, my throbbing cock as I felt every inch of her beneath my hard body. "And then, if you're a good girl, I'll make you come so hard you'll be screaming my name in your dreams."

Her eyes widened, that gorgeous blush darkening.

"No screaming, Hawke," she teased, laughter filling her eyes once more. "We'll scare Santa away, and then he won't leave us any presents!"

She cracked herself up, and I couldn't help but laugh. She was so fucking cute when she laughed, so beautiful.

But cuteness and jokes wouldn't save her. Not tonight.

I leaned in close, nipping her ear and grinding against her, making her gasp.

"Santa lost my address a long time ago, Cupcake. The only present you're getting tonight is my face between your thighs."

I didn't hear what the fuck she said after that, because when I made a promise, I damn well delivered. In a flash, I yanked off her snowman pants and underwear and pressed my mouth to her silky skin, dragging my tongue over her clit. Her thighs clamped around my ears and she fisted my hair, tugging me hard against her center as my mouth claimed that hot, wet flesh in a deep, sensual kiss, her thighs squeezing tighter and tighter, muffling the sounds of her moans.

Fuck that. Those moans were for me, and I needed to hear them. Every delicious sigh and pant and gasp. All of it.

I pulled away and grabbed her thighs, spreading them and pinning them against the couch, taking in the sight of her glistening pussy.

"Fuck, you're beautiful," I whispered. "You're killing me, you know that? I've never wanted anything so fucking bad before, Maddie Lockwood. Not in all my years as a man *or* as a wolf."

I was drunk on her again, dizzy with her scent, with her heat, with my own uncontrollable, untamed need to claim this woman once and for all.

"Hawke..." she breathed, her hips undulating beneath my grip, desperate for more. "You're not... you're not going to tease me again, are you?"

"Depends. Am I forgiven?" I blew a hot breath across her clit, then pressed my lips to it, feathering her with all-too-gentle kisses.

"*Hawke!*"

"Yes or no." I flicked her with my tongue, then gave her a teasing nip, sliding one finger inside her, stroking slowly.

"Not... not fair." She arched her body in a desperate

bid to get closer, but I held back, gently teasing her with my tongue and finger, stopping every time she got too close to the edge, only to start up the endless torture all over again.

"Yes, okay? *Yes!*" She finally caved, grabbing my head and jerking me closer, her eyes blazing. "I forgive you for tonight. I forgive you for everything you've *ever* done. And for anything else you might do or say later. All forgiven. Completely. Slate clean. Just don't tease me anymore because I swear I'm about to lose my—"

I shoved my tongue inside her pussy, cutting her right the fuck off. This time, there was no holding back, no teasing, no stopping. I wanted to make her come hard, just like I'd promised. To come all over my goddamn face.

Maddie fisted my hair, tugging so hard it made my eyes water. She was right there, right on the precipice, her whole body begging me to let her fall.

"Come in my mouth, beautiful," I growled. "Fucking shatter for me."

And then I was right back where I belonged, face buried between her thighs as I tongue-fucked her to ecstasy. She bucked her hips, writhing beneath me, and I kissed and sucked and ate that gorgeous pussy like it was the last thing I'd ever taste, the last time I'd ever have the pleasure of wearing her all over my face.

She came for me with a shuddering cry, and when I finally pulled back and looked into her sweet face, tears glittered on her cheeks.

"Maddie? Are you—"

"Amazing," she said, laughing. "I'm amazing."

"Yeah. You are."

God, she made my fucking mouth water, and I was nowhere near done with her yet.

I didn't even give her a minute to come back down to earth before my mouth found its way back to her inner thigh, slowly kissing a path up to her hipbone. I undid the bottom three buttons of her pajama top, revealing her flat stomach, a cluster of freckles on the left, just below her rib cage. With my tongue, I blazed a trail across her abdomen, licking and kissing my way from one hipbone to the other.

Maddie was still panting, still riding out the aftershocks, but I couldn't wait. Her nipples were hard beneath the shirt, and I wanted those perfect tits in my face, in my mouth. I wanted more of her. All of her. Every freckled inch.

"I need you naked," I said. "Now." I reached for the next button, my stubbled chin grazing the soft skin of her belly as I continued to kiss my way up. That shirt was the very last thing that stood between my mouth and her flesh, and it needed to be gone *yesterday*.

But the second I popped that button, Maddie bolted upright and snatched the fabric out of my hands, hastily refastening her buttons, eyes wide with some deep, inexplicable fear.

And then she opened her mouth and said the one word with the power to put my dick on ice.

"Gingerbread."

MADDIE

Fear was a funny thing.

I was paralyzed on the couch, fingers locked around my buttons, heart slamming against my ribcage.

I'd taken Hawke in my mouth tonight, all the way down. I'd trusted him enough to let him spank me. I'd begged him for more, again and again, and I'd let him explore my most private places, bringing me to ecstasy with every delicious kiss so many times I'd lost count.

Even after he'd freaked out and bailed on me, I'd forgiven him, letting him do all those filthy, beautiful things to me all over again.

Scariest of all? I'd watched him transform from the wolf I thought might eat me into the man who saved my life. A man who'd spent the last hour telling me all the monsters in the movies were real. That some of them were even my clients.

But none of that had frightened me away.

Only this.

This one ridiculously small, inconsequential thing was the thing that'd stopped me in dead my tracks and forced that silly little safe word out of my mouth.

He'd tried to take off my shirt.

"Maddie?" Hawke cupped my face, his stormy gray eyes filled with a mix of concern and confusion. "Damn, you're shaking. You're scared out of your mind." Guilt replaced the confusion in his eyes. "We don't have to do anything you're not one hundred percent comfortable with—that's why I gave you the safe word. There's no need to be scared."

"I know. It's not... it's not that."

"What did I do?" he asked, scrubbing a hand over his jaw. "Jesus, Maddie. Tell me so I can fix this. Whatever it is, let me fix it. Please."

"Hawke. You didn't do anything wrong." I closed the distance between us, climbing into his lap and straddling him, the cold metal of his button and zipper an exquisite shock against my bare flesh.

God, he was so hard for me.

The aftershocks of his touch lingered; I was still so

wound up for him—no matter how intense my fears—and I needed him to know it.

I curled my hands over his shoulders and smiled, trying to be brave. Trying to find the words to explain something I barely understood myself.

"I want you," I whispered. "Please believe it. It's just…"

Hawke ran his hands up my back, burying them in my hair. When I still didn't finish my thought, he said, "I'd give anything to know what's was going on in that head of yours, Cupcake. Anything in the world."

"It's… kind of a long story."

"Everything with you is kind of a long story." He smiled and touched his forehead to mine. "Besides, I told you mine, right? So maybe it's time you tell me yours. I'm not going anywhere. I promise."

I nodded and took a deep, steadying breath, trying to decide where to start.

Reaching inside my snowman top, I fished out my heart locket, opening it up so Hawke could see the inside. There were no pictures, no jewels. Only names, one engraved on each side.

Madison on the left.

Rachel on the right.

Hawke held the locket between his thumb and forefinger, turning it so he could read it in the firelight. "Who's Rachel?"

"She died," I said. "Skiing accident last December twentieth. I was in a coma at the time—for about a week at that point."

"What?" He dropped the locked and shifted his hands to my hips, holding me tight, his gaze turning fierce. "What the hell happened?"

"The last thing I remember was my parents standing on either side of my hospital bed, both of them in tears. They'd flown in that night—the doctor came in and told them to prepare for the worst. They didn't think I was conscious at the time, but I heard every word. Doc said I wouldn't survive the week."

I closed my eyes, shivering at the memories of those dark days. But I had to keep going, had to get this out. I wanted Hawke to know me, and this was my story, part of who I was just like the wolf was part of him—part of the long and winding roads that eventually brought us here.

I told him how I'd been born with a congenital heart defect, and after defying all the doctors' predictions and living beyond my first year of life, I spent my entire childhood battling illness, infection, tests, weakness, germs, fear, needles, pain. Doctors were always telling my parents to prepare for the worst, but even at my lowest points, I'd bounced back every time, sometimes even stronger than the last.

"But," I continued, "last year was different. Something inside me had changed irreparably, and for the first time in my life, I knew the doctors were right. My heart was finally giving out, and no amount of machinery or medication could keep it beating. I was at a client's holiday party in SoHo when I passed out and hit my head, and when I woke up, I was in the hospital, connected to dozens of tubes and machines. I didn't even have the strength to lift my head off the pillow, to tell them I was still there, to say my goodbyes. My parents held my hands as the doctor's news settled over the room like a cold, dark shadow, and then everything went black."

"Holy shit, Maddie."

"When I finally came to again," I said, "I thought I was dead. I opened my eyes and all I saw was a bright, white light. I thought I was supposed to follow it—that's what everyone says, right?" I laughed. "But it turns out it was just my window. There was a storm in New York City, snow blowing all sideways and crazy like it is tonight. It was Christmas day. They wouldn't let my family in yet, but the doctors and nurses were there. They said I'd flatlined three times, but they brought me back, and now it looked like I was here to stay. The surgeon told me I had a new scar for my collection, and underneath it, the heart of a seventeen-year-old girl beating inside my chest."

I grabbed Hawke's hand and slid it inside my shirt, pressing it to my bare chest. To my scar and the wild heart beating beneath it. "I guess I was just... I don't know. Afraid to let you see it. Afraid of what you'd think."

Hawke didn't say anything at first, just sat with me, warm hand pressed to my bare skin, his eyes full of emotion.

When he finally spoke, it was barely a whisper. "Do you really think you're any less beautiful to me—any less incredible—because of a scar?"

"No, not like that. It's..." I closed my eyes, trying to find a way to explain it. To put my jumbled thoughts into words. "You were right, all that stuff you said before. I *love* the way you touch me. The things you do to me. The way you make me feel. When I'm with you, when you're touching me like that, you don't hold back. I feel *everything*. And I guess I just..." I blew out a breath, my heart ramping up again, that old fear rising inside. "You're this strong, amazing, super-powerful wolf shifter who can stand naked in the middle of a blizzard without getting so much as chapped lips, and I'm... I'm a human woman who needs someone else's heart and a dozen pills a day just to stay alive. I guess I was scared you'd see my scar and think I was sick or weak—like I wouldn't be able to handle the way you've been touching me. And then you'd stop touching me altogether, which—"

Hawke fisted my hair and claimed me with a bruising kiss, so wild and ferocious it hurt. When he finally pulled away, my lips were swollen, and both of us were panting.

"Madison Lockwood, you are the strongest, most fierce, most stubborn, most passionate, most incredible, craziest, most pain-in-the-ass woman I've ever met. *Nothing* could change my mind about that." He pressed his hand flat against my chest again, his eyes blazing in the firelight. "You have someone else's heart beating in your chest, and you're fucking *alive* because of it. You're *here* because of it. You survived. *That's* what this scar means—survival. Not sickness. Not weakness. Survival. So wear it like a fucking badge of honor, because that's what it is."

Keeping his gaze locked on mine, Hawke ran his fingers along the thick red ridge bisecting my chest, marking the great *before* and *after* of my life. Before, I couldn't walk up a flight of stairs without stopping to rest. I couldn't hike with my family in the Colorado summers. I couldn't play hide-and-seek with my nieces or go whitewater rafting or meet my friends anywhere in New York without flagging down a taxi, even if it was just three blocks away.

But after?

After, I could breathe again. After, I could run. I could hike. I could live.

I could love.

Hawke was right—my scar *was* a badge of honor.

In that moment, sitting in his lap, my hands warm on his broad shoulders, I smiled for the girl whose heart now beat in my chest, and I wondered if she'd ever been in love. If this very heart had ever beat so wildly, so passionately for another person.

I hoped it had. I sensed it knew what it was doing. That it wouldn't let me down.

I thought again of the North star. The bright light in the storm. My Christmas wish.

I'd been given another second chance tonight—with my life. With Hawke.

Now, all I had to do was reach out and take it.

MADDIE

There was a question in Hawke's eyes, and I answered him with another smile, silently nodding and lowering my arms.

He took his time removing my shirt, unbuttoning each button, unwrapping me like a precious gift. That's what it felt like—like I was giving him something special, some part of myself I'd never before shared with another man, saved up all this time just for him.

He slid the shirt off my shoulders and marveled at me, unabashed.

"You're so damn beautiful, Maddie," Hawke whispered, his lips brushing the corner of my mouth, his hands trailing lightly over my breasts, sending me into a full-bodied shiver. "Your bright blue eyes. Your crazy hair. Your mouth. Your perfect ass. And especially this."

He trailed his lips down the line of my scar from the base of my throat to my diaphragm, painting it with slow, fevered kisses that left me breathless. "I want my mouth on every part of you."

"Me too." I unzipped his hoodie and slid it off his shoulders, unwrapping him just as he'd unwrapped me—a gift to be cherished. He slid his arms out, and the hoodie fell to the couch, revealing his full torso to me.

I'd seen him naked earlier tonight, but that was different. That was standing in the dark forest in the middle of a snowstorm, still trying to reconcile the fact that I'd seen a wolf shift into a man before my eyes.

Now, before the warm, flickering glow of the fire, I could actually look at him. *Really* look at him.

His skin was a map of scars—too many to count. The deep slash of a knife wound along his ribcage. Two white circles on his right shoulder that had to be bullet wounds. Beneath them, an angry red X that could only be from a brand.

We rose together from the couch, and Hawke slid out of his jeans and boxers, revealing more of the same. Angry silver scars and slashes on his thigh, his legs. Knives and teeth. Whips and fire. Pain and torture.

My throat tightened, my vision blurring with tears. I wanted to kiss away every last mark, every last bit of pain he'd ever experienced, inside and out.

"I'm still here," Hawke said softly. "I survived, just like you. That's all it means. That's all it's ever meant." He dipped his head and recaptured my gaze, then kissed me, sucking my lip between his teeth, biting gently, our breaths mingling as I sighed into his mouth and gave in to this pleasure one more time.

My eyes fluttered closed as Hawke's hands slid down to cup my ass, and beneath his expert touch, the last of my reservations melted away.

Right now, all that existed was us, scarred and imperfect, but whole and alive, brought together by fate for one incredible, life-changing night before Christmas.

His addicting evergreens-and-cinnamon scent enveloped me as he kissed my shoulder, my neck, my collarbone, tracing a path to my breasts with his mouth. His dark hair tickled my skin as he grazed my nipple with his teeth, then licked, rough and then soft, the opposing sensations driving me wild with desire.

He ran his fingers down my chest, my abdomen, and instinctively I parted my thighs for him, welcoming his commanding touch once more. With a low growl, he dipped two fingers inside me, his thumb rubbing agonizingly slow circles against my clit, his mouth everywhere at once, kissing my scar, my nipples.

Hawke made love to my breasts the same way he'd

made love to my mouth, to my thighs, to my stomach, as if every inch of my flesh was something to be worshipped. He was passionate, he was wild, he was so damn sensual.

And he never, ever treated me like glass.

"You feel so good," I whispered, losing myself to the hot pleasure of his tongue. It was perfect and exquisite, but suddenly, it wasn't enough.

Suddenly, I didn't want to come by his fingers or his mouth.

I wanted him inside me. Now.

I sank down onto the plush rug in front of the fireplace, pulling Hawke down on top of me, his hard, delicious cock pressing against my abdomen.

He cupped my face, kissing my chin, my jaw, my ear. In a hot, soft breath, he whispered, "Touch yourself for me, Maddie."

I was powerless to resist. I didn't *want* to resist. I wanted to do everything he asked, everything he demanded.

Because everything he demanded felt so damn right.

"I used to be a nice girl before I met you." I laughed softly as my hand drifted down between us.

"That a fact?" Hawke asked.

"No spankings," I whispered, running a finger across my clit. "No orgasms at the dinner table."

"Sounds like you met me just in time."

I closed my eyes, the pleasure of my own touch making me shiver. "And now I have a naughty side."

Hawke was rock-hard for me, throbbing against my thigh as he watched me stroke myself. I'd never been so hot and wet before, so desperate for a man's touch.

No, not just a man's touch. Hawke's *touch.*

I craved him. *Needed* him. My legs fell open as I slid my fingers into my own slick heat and imagined Hawke thrusting inside me.

"Your naughty side is very, *very* nice," he teased, pressing a hot kiss to my mouth.

I melted beneath his soft lips, his kiss at once gentle and fierce.

"Hawke," I moaned. "I'm too close. I need you inside me before I—"

"Not yet, Cupcake." He grabbed my hand and sucked my fingers into his mouth, stopping the momentum of my impending explosion.

I opened my eyes. I was so tight and wound up, so desperate, so delirious. I arched my hips to get closer, begging him to slide inside, but still he made me wait, swirling his hot, velvet tongue over my fingertips, watching me with intense hunger, with desire, with his own desperate need flooding his eyes.

"Tell me what you want," he said, sliding my fingers

from his mouth. He kissed my wrist, the inside of my elbow, the edge of my armpit, his cock pressing eagerly against my thigh, close, but not close enough. "Tell me what you need."

"You," I said, breathless. "I need you inside me."

"Inside *where*, my naughty, beautiful Cupcake?"

I whimpered softly, my heart racing as the fire in my belly churned and roiled.

I'd meant what I told him—I'd never played like this before. No dirty talk, no touching myself, no spankings, none of it. Twenty-four hours ago, I would've blushed at the very thought.

But this man, this *wolf*, had unlocked something inside me—something wild and dangerous, something uninhibited.

Something I was only just beginning to explore.

Something I really, really liked.

"Tell me where you want me." Hawke's eyes were full of fire as he finally positioned himself at my entrance, teasing me with the tip, another growl rumbling through his chest, and for the first time in my life, I felt truly powerful. Strong. Beautiful. Confident. Unstoppable.

And sexy as hell.

With a wave of renewed confidence, I parted my thighs wider and said, "I want you to *own* me, Hawke.

Own this hot, wet pussy. It's yours."

Hawke growled again and grabbed my wrists, pinning them to the floor above my head. In a deep, gravelly voice that made my stomach flip, he ground out, "You're already mine, Maddie. Every part of you. *Mine.*"

Without warning, he slammed into me, fierce and deep, filling me so completely I could no longer tell where I ended and Hawke began.

He smothered my mouth with another bruising kiss, one powerful hand clamped around my wrists, his other gliding down my body past the curve of my ass, grabbing my thigh and guiding my leg over his shoulder, thrusting in even deeper.

Hawke was crazy with lust, with need, growling and baring his teeth like an animal as he rode me harder and faster, grinding my hips and shoulders into the rug, the fire making everything that much hotter between us, that much more slippery.

The sensation of his hard body sliding against my flesh sent electric tingles up my spine and across my shoulders, and I didn't want it to end.

Not tonight. Not tomorrow night. Not ever.

"I need to feel you," I breathed against his lips. Begged. "I need to touch you."

Hawke released my wrists, and I ran my hands down his back, his muscles rippling beneath my touch as he grew even harder for me, my body stretching to accommodate him.

Holy hell, yes.

I sank my fingers into his firm ass, urging him closer, rolling my hips as we found our perfect rhythm, sliding together and apart, taking and giving, feeling and touching and tasting every bit of each other until I was right back at that precipice, hanging on by a gossamer thread.

"Let go, Maddie," Hawke said. "Let it all fucking go. Come for me."

Those words were my undoing.

A wave of heat flooded my core, and I arched my body and took him in even deeper, my strong and beautiful heart hammering inside as I dug my nails into Hawke's back and shattered beneath him with a thunderous cry ripped from my very soul, taking with it every last one of my inhibitions, my what-ifs, my fears.

Pure, unadulterated pleasure crashed through me, lighting me up from the inside as Hawke slammed into me. He was right there with me, and he grabbed my shoulders and let out one last feral growl, his whole body shuddering with the force of his orgasm as he emptied himself completely, both of us riding the same delicious wave to the edge of eternity.

When it was finally over, Hawke collapsed against my chest, our bodies slick with sweat.

His hair tickled my nose, and I let it fall into my mouth as I held him close. I wanted to capture this moment, to remember it always.

"You okay?" he asked, breath raw and ragged against my chest.

I laughed. I was *more* than okay. I was a damn phoenix rising out of the ashes of my old life, renewed and remade. Strong and beautiful. On fire.

Hawke had given me that gift.

He'd marked me. Changed me. Unlocked me. And in that moment, tangled up and trembling on the floor in a snowbound cabin at the top of the sky, I made a permanent place for him in my heart.

2 5

HAWKE

Christmas morning dawned way too early, the bright Colorado sun streaming in through the wooden blinds in my bedroom. I hadn't even fully opened my eyes yet, but I was already hard as fuck, still dreaming about all the things I'd done last night with that gorgeous, fiery redhead.

Nothing in my life had ever felt so good. So right.

She'd been so warm and soft in my arms, her lean body perfectly aligned against my chest, my fingers tangled up in her crazy curls as we made love again and again, both of us spent and happy when we'd finally drifted off to sleep.

It'd been the most peaceful night's sleep I'd gotten in a decade.

I turned onto my side now and reached for her, aching to tangle my hands in those curls again, to bury myself between her thighs...

But the sheets beside me were cold.

I opened my eyes, heart in my damn throat.

My woman was gone.

Well. Ain't that *a bitch of a way to wake up on Christmas.*

I sat up and rubbed the sleep from my eyes, trying to breathe through that hollowed-out feeling inside me.

But there, stacked up in the corner of my room like it belonged there, was Maddie's endless supply of luggage.

She hadn't left me yet.

The breath whooshed out of my lungs, and I shook my head, laughing at myself.

When the fuck did you become such a lightweight, Stevens? Fuck.

One night with Maddie Lockwood, and I'd gone completely soft.

I fisted my cock.

Okay, maybe not completely *soft...*

But hell, I wasn't about to stand around with my dick in my hand. Not when there was a beautiful woman somewhere in this cabin.

I threw on a hoodie and a pair of flannel pajama

pants and opened my blinds, checking out the scene. It was a damn winter wonderland out there, everything covered in a thick, white blanket that sparkled in the sun. It felt like the world had been scrubbed clean and given a second chance.

Too bad it can't last...

Darkness banged on the door of my heart, but I locked it down. I still had some time with her. Maybe an hour. Maybe a minute. Either way, I wasn't about to waste another *second* dwelling on that inevitable goodbye.

But first...

Digging through a box of old shit shoved into the very back of my closet, I retrieved the one thing—other than my mouth—guaranteed to put a smile on my girl's face.

Santa hat, leftover from one of my last Christmases with my mom and sister. It was one of the few things I'd held on to from those days, and now I was glad I hadn't pitched it into the trash with the rest of the stuff.

For so long, all those old memories brought only pain and darkness. It was long past time to change that.

Downstairs, a new fire was crackling in the hearth. The power had been restored sometime in the night, and now the whole place smelled like breakfast. Not watery oatmeal and a protein shake spiked with a shot of whiskey, but a real, homemade, loosen-up-your-pants-and-spend-the-whole-damn-day-in-a-food-coma breakfast.

"What kind of trouble are you two getting into down here?" I asked my girls.

"Good morning, sleepyhead," Maddie said, not turning away from the stove. Wearing nothing but one of my flannel shirts and a pair of hiking socks that went up over her knees, my girl was happily frying up some bacon, her red hair all over the damn place. Bella lay curled up on the floor at Maddie's feet, gnawing on her favorite bone, happy as a pig in shit.

The storm had passed. The lights were back on. The fire was blazing. I'd enjoyed the most mind-blowing sex of my life last night. My dog was happy. And there was a hot, half-naked woman frying up bacon in my kitchen.

Christmas was looking better by the minute.

"Ah, Cupcake," I said, joining her at the stove and sliding my hands around her hips. "Where have you been all my life?"

"No idea, but you almost missed it. You sleep like a bear. Well, I guess a wolf makes more sense in this context. Do wolves sleep like bears? Or is that not a thing?"

"You wore me out last night, woman. What the hell did you expect?"

Maddie finally turned around to look at me, and when she spotted the Santa hat, her eyebrows jumped up, her eyes brightened about ten shades, and that megawatt kid-on-Christmas grin of hers stretched across her face.

And the very last chunk of ice cracked and fell right off my heart.

"Don't say a word," I teased, pressing my finger to her lips. "Or it's gone."

"I'm not saying a word. Just... Merry Christmas. Am I allowed to say that?"

"I suppose I can make an exception for that." Grinning, I leaned in close and stole a sweet good-morning kiss.

"Bacon!" she shouted suddenly, pulling away and turning her attention back to the frying pan. "You have to watch it, or it'll burn."

As she tended to her bacon, I looked around the kitchen, noticing all the other work she'd done. Not only had she brought in more wood for the fire, but the table was covered in hot, fresh food—cheesy eggs with broccoli and red pepper, hash browns, a stack of pancakes a mile high, fresh-squeezed orange juice, coffee. She'd even made a centerpiece out of emergency candles and a cluster of pinecones and boughs she must've collected from outside.

"Maddie, you... You did all this?" My damn eyes watered. Girl must've chopped up some onions in those eggs, or maybe it was the candle smoke. Had to be something like that.

"Since you gave the head chef the week off, I kind of had to." Maddie laughed, and I tried desperately to hold on to it, to memorize the sound. "I know you're not into Christmas trees or anything, but I figured you wouldn't mind if I improvised on a few decorations. Bella helped me pick them out. Didn't you, girl? After you chased that poor fox through the snow, you big goofball."

The dog barked, wagging her tail like she'd just been awarded a medal of honor.

"Oh, by the way," Maddie said, "you really shouldn't keep the emergency flares in the same box as the candles. You almost got a very *different* kind of wakeup call. And I couldn't find any pepper, so I had to get the little packets out of those... those army TV dinners, or whatever they are. You've got some weird stuff in there, Hawke. Honestly."

"MREs," I said, grinning my ass off. Why was she so fucking cute?

"Well, whatever they're called, the next time you try to eat one, you won't have any pepper. I left the salt, though. But I think they're mostly expired, anyway. You should probably just—"

"I should probably just..." I slid an arm around her waist, stroking the curve of her ass. The soft little moan escaping her mouth made me instantly hard again, but more than that, she just felt... right. *Damn* right in my arms. Right wearing my shirt. Right filling my kitchen with the sound of her sweet voice and laughter. Right cooking breakfast on Christmas morning as if she'd been meant to find her way to my doorstep all along.

"You're a crazy girl," I said, burying my face in the crook of her neck, inhaling her scent. "A crazy, sexy, incredible girl who crashed into my driveway and turned my whole fucking world upside down in a single night."

"Hey! You're the one who told me shifters and vampires are real. Talk about turning the whole world upside down in a single night."

"Guess that makes us even, right?"

"How do you figure?"

I laughed. "Now we *both* believe in fairy tales."

"Wow, all that in a single night." Maddie smirked. "Imagine what we could do with an entire week?"

"I couldn't keep up with you for an entire week, Cupcake."

But fuck if I didn't want to. A week, a month, my whole damn life.

All this time, I'd merely been existing. Living life from the wrong side of the window, just like she'd said. But then Maddie literally crashed into my life, and suddenly I felt alive again, seeing everything around me in vivid color instead of drab shades of gray.

Somehow, despite my best efforts, the woman had found a way in, breeching my walls, jackhammering the ice right off my heart.

The thought of letting her walk out that door today carved me open inside, damn near gutting me.

I thought I'd be okay saying goodbye; from the very start, I knew she'd be out of here as soon as the storm broke, and we'd given each other one hell of a sendoff last night.

But now that the hour of her imminent departure was closing in, I couldn't fucking bear it. I didn't want to know what tonight would feel like without her in my arms. What *I* would feel like.

Maybe it was crazy, but hell—just like the existence of shifters and vampires and all the other creatures that went bump in the night—what Maddie and I had was real. Didn't matter that I'd only met her a day ago. Sometimes, you just fucking *knew*.

I lifted her hair and pressed my nose to the back of

her bare neck, inhaling her sweet scent once more, stirring the possessive, protective wolf inside me to life.

I knew the reality, knew my words wouldn't change it for either of us. But I had to say them anyway, because if there was anyone listening—any fucking North star, Santa Claus, Christmas miracle magic left to make it happen—I had to give it a shot.

"Stay with me, Cupcake," I whispered. "Just stay."

MADDIE

I'll miss you, girl." I pressed a kiss to Bella's nose and rubbed behind her ears. "Keep your daddy in line for me, okay? Don't take any shit from him, no matter what."

Bella barked and licked my face, wagging her cute little doggy-butt like today was just the best day ever.

I couldn't argue with her. Other than the goodbye on the horizon, it really *had* been the best day. The best night. The best of a lot of things, all thanks to one sexy-as-hell, crazy-ass mountain wolf.

We'd taken our time with breakfast, sneaking a kiss here, a touch there as we worked our way through the feast. We talked and laughed, even as Hawke's earlier words still hung between us—a question unanswered, potential unmet.

Stay with me, Cupcake...

Holy snowballs, how I wanted to. More than anything.

Our night had been the most amazing of my life. Hidden beneath the snow, time had stopped for us, and somehow we'd found ourselves together, suspended in one beautiful, frozen moment. A perfect snow globe fantasy.

But the sun had risen this morning, bringing real life right along with it. The power and phones were back online, and soon the tow truck would be here. I'd called my parents to let them know I was in town and would be there soon. I was all packed up, dressed once again in my elf costume, excited to spend some time with my family.

By this time tomorrow, I'd be heading back to Denver, then boarding a plane for New York, supernatural capital of the world—a thing I still hadn't completely processed. And Hawke, my wolf, my mountain man... He'd be here, two thousand miles away from my bed. From my heart.

I gave Bella one more kiss and a belly rub for good measure, then stood up to say the big goodbye. The one that was going to hurt the worst, because everything that came before it had been the best.

"I'm still deciding whether or not I'll miss *you*," I

teased. I stood on my tiptoes and looped my arms around Hawke's neck. "A little bit, maybe."

"Hmm. Don't I get a belly rub, too?"

"Is that what my big, bad wolf needs? A belly rub?"

"You tell me." He grabbed my hand and slid it up inside his hoodie, pressing it against his hot, firm abs.

I sighed. I'd be dreaming about the rock-hard ridges and planes of his body for years to come. The muscles. The scars. The stories. And yes, his wolf form, too—beautiful and majestic. Powerful. A miracle that stole my breath away every time I remembered the sight of it.

"Pretty sure you got enough of a rubdown last night," I said, forcing some levity into my voice. I didn't want to leave with tears in my eyes, no matter how badly it hurt.

"When it comes to you, Cupcake, I'll never get enough." Hawke dipped his head low and captured my mouth in a kiss, a gentle brush of lips that quickly deepened, turning hungry and all-consuming. It was the kind of kiss I felt all the way to my toes, my heart beating its strong, now-familiar beat.

Don't go, it seemed to say. *Don't go. Don't go. Don't go. Don't go...*

I pulled back, taking his face into my hands, memorizing the feel of his stubbled jaw, the look of fire in his fierce, flint-gray eyes. "You, um... You kinda saved my life last night, Hawke."

He touched his forehead to mine, his whispers falling hot on my lips. "You kinda saved mine, too."

I kissed him again, then pressed my ear to his chest, listening to the strong, solid beat of his heart as he palmed the back of my head, his touch warm and protective.

The tears I'd been trying so hard to keep at bay finally spilled.

It all seemed so unfair.

I'd grown up in Colorado never having crossed Hawke's path, and now I lived in New York City. He'd traversed the globe a dozen times over, and now he lived here, in a cabin high up in the Rockies. If not for a freak of nature, an unintentional detour on the road of life, we would've continued on our separate paths never having met.

But now that fate had brought us together, Hawke would always be a part of my life, even if only as a memory—one pristine, perfect evening when the world was sound asleep beneath the snow and I was safe and happy in his arms.

I didn't want Hawke as a memory, though. I wanted the real thing. And now, no matter how many times I tried to pull away from his heartbeat, to let him go, I couldn't.

We just felt *right* together. Like we'd been given a once-in-a-lifetime shot at something truly great.

I didn't know how to make it work—whether humans and supernaturals could be together, whether we could overcome the distance and the differences in our lives, whether it even made sense to try.

All I knew for sure was that if I walked out that door now without telling him how I felt, it would become the single biggest regret in my entire life.

No more living on the wrong side of the window, Maddie. You promised. Remember?

"Hawke," I said, still listening to the steady thump of his heart. "I know it's crazy, but... Okay, I'm just going to put it out there. Here it is: I don't want to say goodbye."

"Yeah, well." Hawke sighed, warm breath stirring my hair. "Maybe I don't want to say goodbye either." He pulled me tighter against the solid wall of his chest, locking me in his embrace. "Maybe I want to keep you here for lunch. And then drive you to your parents' place later. And then pick you up after dinner and bring you back here and keep you a little longer. A *lot* longer. Maybe that's what I want."

My heart skipped into a frantic beat, my nerves buzzing, skin flush with new warmth.

"Maybe that's what I want, too," I said. "But maybe... maybe I don't want you to just drive me to my parents' place. Maybe... maybe I want you to come in and have dinner with us. Maybe I want you to meet my family, which is *completely* nuts because yes, I know, we only just met each other last night and you don't do families and—"

"Maddie?" He hooked a finger under my chin and grinned down at me, the sight nearly stopping my heart. "Twenty-four hours ago, I didn't do Christmas, either. Yet here I stand wearing a goddamn Santa hat and getting all weepy over some pine branches on my kitchen table. So hell, maybe I do families now, too. Maybe I do families because it's important to you, and it would mean getting to spend a few more hours with you I otherwise wouldn't get. Maybe I do families now because maybe, just maybe, it feels like you're *my* family."

"Hawke," I breathed, emotion tightening my throat. "I... I don't know what to say."

"Say you'll stay. Say you'll help me figure out what comes next."

"But..." My voice trembled, everything inside me buzzing and hot. "But how?"

Hawke pulled me in close again and pressed his lips to the top of my head. I fit there in his arms so snugly, so perfectly, it was as if that spot was made just for me. Like he'd been waiting all these years for me to show up and take my place.

"Dunno," he said. "But that's the thing—twenty-four hours ago? I *did* know. I knew *exactly* what my life was all about. I knew how every damn day would start. How every night would end. Then out of fucking *nowhere*, this hot, redheaded little elf shows up on my doorstep on Christmas Eve and gives my entire world a spin. Nothing makes sense anymore, and I don't need it to. All I need is you, Maddie. All I need is for you to tell me you feel it, too. That you're willing to give us a real shot. And if you're not, if I'm way off base here? Then I need you to look me in the eye, say gingerbread, and put me out of my misery."

I pulled back to meet his gaze, searching his eyes for the slightest hint that this was all just a ruse, just another naughty-wolf tease.

But all I found in those flint-gray eyes was sincerity. Vulnerability. A truth that reached right inside my chest and lit up my heart.

It took me a minute to catch my breath. To get my mouth to form words. Then, finally, with a grin that stretched from ear to ear, I said, "The only way I'm ever saying the G-word again is if we're making cookies. I'm in, Hawke."

"Yeah?" A smile, soft and shy. Relieved.

"Yeah."

That was all he needed to hear.

Hawke crushed his lips against mine, claiming me in a possessive kiss that left no room for interpretation. I moaned into his mouth, my legs going weak as he threaded his fingers into my hair.

When he finally pulled back, he was laughing, a sound that reverberated through his entire body. "Damn, woman. You left me hanging for so long, I wasn't sure I was still breathing." Cupping my face in his big, strong hands, he said, "I don't give a fuck how crazy it sounds or how far apart we live. I told you this last night, and I meant it. You're *mine*, Cupcake. Non-negotiable."

"It's that simple, then?"

"Simple, complicated, impossible. Doesn't matter. It's the way it's gonna be. But Maddie?" His gaze turned feral, sending a spark of desire straight to my core. He backed me up against the wall and kissed the corner of my mouth, slowly making his way across my jaw to my ear as his hands wandered down my arms, my hips, finally dipping under my dress. "That architect roommate of yours? He's gotta *go*."

"What?" I laughed. "You've got nothing to worry

about there—*his* A-game sucks. Derrick has never once made me Alfredo sauce."

"And now he never will, because he's leaving. What a fucking tragedy."

I didn't argue. I didn't care. Right now, all I cared about was Hawke's mouth on my neck, his rough, demanding fingers slipping inside my panties, stroking me until my legs trembled.

"Hawke Stevens," I panted, quickly losing my ability to form words. "You're so... oh my God, you're so *naughty*."

"You ain't seen nothing yet." He pushed his fingers in deeper, thrusting in and out, slowly massaging my clit with his thumb. Heat gathered between my thighs, pulsing outward until everything in me felt hot and slippery. "Just wait until I get you naked again."

"Why wait?" I hooked a finger into one of the stockings, sliding it down my thigh.

"Ah, *nope*." Hawke grabbed my wrist and tugged the stocking right back up again. "Not happening."

"But I was—"

"Sorry." He flashed a wicked smile that sent another electric jolt to my core. "The candy-cane tights stay on today, Cupcake. You just close your eyes and let me worry about the rest."

I had no choice but to obey, leaning my head back

against the wall as Hawke dropped to his knees and buried his head under my dress. He slid his fingers out of me slowly, then filled his hands with my ass, his tongue tracing a slow, torturous pattern from the inside of one thigh to the other, hot breath ghosting over the triangle of my panties, teasing me as only Hawke could.

I loved his teasing, though. Loved his touch. And I was so, so grateful for every happy accident that had brought me careening into his driveway—into his life.

"You taste so fucking good," Hawke growled. "I'll never stop craving you." He bit the lacy edge of my panties, pulling them down my thighs, unwrapping me once again. His mouth on my sensitive skin was warm and soft, but I knew what was coming next, and there would be nothing soft about it.

With Hawke, nothing was ever going to be soft. But it was *good*. And now, it was all mine.

Like so much in life, this thing unfolding between us came with no guarantees. But it brought the promise of a brand new adventure—the kind of passionate, reckless, beautiful, wild unknown that made my heart sing.

I slid my hands into his hair and lost myself to the feel of Hawke's mouth, his touch, his breath, his promises, each one sealed with a red-hot kiss that would leave me smoldering for the rest of forever, inside and out.

Not even Santa himself could've given me a more perfect Christmas gift.

Thank you so much for reading Hawke and Maddie's story in SNOWED IN WITH THE WOLF!

If you enjoy spicy-hot paranormal romance, you definitely need to meet the Redthorne royal vampires Hawke mentioned and see what kind of delicious trouble those sexy-as-sin bloodsuckers are causing in New York City!

If you're new to the Vampire Royals of New York world, start with book one of Dorian's trilogy, **DARK DECEPTION.** If you're tuning in after finishing Dorian's story, jump into Gabriel's bed—I mean, BOOKS! Jump into Gabriel's books!—with **HEART OF THORNS.**

Read on for an excerpt from Dark Deception. Not from chapter one—I wanted to give you something you wouldn't find in the preview on the bookstore websites —but they're not spoilery. Just a couple snippets that show us *exactly* what kind of vampires we're dealing with here.

Oh, and there's one *very* important thing you should know about the Redthorne brothers before diving in...

They're British. And that accent? As they say all those oh-so-filthy words to their women?

Panty. Melting.

So... yeah. Carry on, then. And happy reading!

Are you a member of our private Facebook group, <u>Sarah Piper's Sassy Witches?</u> Pop in for sneak peeks, cover reveals, exclusive giveaways, book chats, group therapy to deal with these killer cliffhangers, and plenty of complete randomness from your fellow fans! We'd love to see you there.

XOXO
Sarah

"I'll keep *all* your secrets, love." Dorian covered the woman's delicate fingers, holding her hand firmly against his chest. "Though I strongly caution you against deceiving me."

She gazed up at him through dark, feathery lashes and bit her lower lip, likely buying more time to invent her excuse. The woman was no louse in the fine art of seduction, and she was clearly up to no good. But what *kind* of no good, Dorian could only speculate. Robbery was top of his mind, but if that were the case, she had very few options for hiding her treasure; that hot little dress was definitely *not* made for smuggling.

"I have reason to believe the family is on the verge of bankruptcy," she finally said. "I heard they might consider offers for pieces not officially on the block."

Dorian laughed. "Considering what I paid for that painting, it's likely they're back in the black."

"Three million dollars? Doubtful. That's a drop in the bucket for these people."

"*These* people?" He raised an eyebrow, gaze sweeping up from her designer shoes to the tasteful but nevertheless authentic diamonds studding her earlobes. The woman even *smelled* rich—a combination of scents so firmly embedded in his mind it would follow him through eternity.

Who did she think she was fooling?

"I just meant..." She closed her mouth and pulled away from his grasp, doing her best to mask her irritation. When she spoke again, her voice had softened considerably. "It's a terrible situation. They have a lot of debt. The penthouse is in foreclosure. They're actually moving overseas."

Trading gossip about other people's misfortunes was beneath him, but he suspected her theory was true. He'd been gouged on the painting, but they would've settled for a lot less if she and Duchanes hadn't run up the bidding.

"I fail to see what their financial situation has to do with your sneaking around."

"It has everything to do with it," she snapped, her cheeks blushing with frustration and more than a little arousal. "But nothing to do with *you*. So if you don't mind, please show yourself out."

"You expect me to turn my back on a potential crime in progress?"

"I expect you to... Look, I totally appreciate the earlier save. Who knows what that creep would've done if you hadn't ridden in on your white horse? And thanks for the drinks, and the fun conversation, and..." She closed her eyes and blew out a breath, shaking her head as if she were having an argument with her own mind.

Dorian wasn't sure who won, but when she looked at him again, her eyes blazed with fresh anger.

"But seriously," she said. "It doesn't concern you."

"I see." Dorian offered a wry smile. Trouble or not, her feistiness turned him on beyond reason. The attitude, the taser, the spark of disobedience in her eyes...

You need to be tied up and spanked, little prowler.

Blood and power hummed through his veins, the image of his handprint on her bare flesh igniting a different sort of hunger inside.

This long into an immortal life, there were few things Dorian still enjoyed. The company of a beautiful woman was, on occasion, one of them.

But nothing—*nothing*—made him harder than a woman with fire. A woman who could hold her own, even as she begged to be dominated.

Soon enough, he'd have her doing both.

He took a step toward her, the soft thud of her pulse an erotic drumbeat that damn near hypnotized him.

For a moment, her anger faded, and she held his gaze in silence, tension crackling between them, her breath shallow, mouth slightly parted. She bit her bottom lip again, and he stared eagerly, already imagining the sweet taste of her kiss, the dangerous tease of her blood as his fangs grazed the plump flesh...

"The painting," she said suddenly, breaking the trance. She turned toward the fireplace, gesturing at the art displayed over the mantle. "Heinrich von Hausen's *Adrift*. One of his lesser known works, but still a masterpiece by any measure."

"You'll have to try harder than that," he said. "You've already impressed me with your knowledge of art."

"I'm not trying to impress you. I'm trying to tell you

that *this* painting is one of my favorites. My father took me to see it at the Smithsonian when I was a kid. How it ended up here, I can only imagine. But as soon as I saw it, I knew I wanted to ask the owners about it. Maybe arrange for a private bid, or... I don't know. Something."

An echo of sadness lingered in her voice, as raw and authentic as the painting itself, chased by a wave of the same darkness he'd seen earlier, rising anew in her eyes.

If he'd met her a hundred years ago—fifty, even— maybe he would've asked her about it. Offered comfort. Promises. Hell, maybe he'd have marched right back into the auction room, tracked down the host, and bought the damn painting for her on the spot, just to make her smile.

But these days, there was no room in his heart for sentimentality.

Only hunger.

Only desire.

In a flash, he closed the last of the distance between them, forcing her to take a step back, then another. Her shoulders hit the door of a small closet, and she dropped her purse and gasped, looking up at him with a mix of fear and lust, a combination that all but sealed her fate.

"Touching story." He trailed a finger across her exposed collarbone. Not far below, the curve of her breasts peaked out over the top of her dress, full and inviting. It was another of her many contradictions—hot and hard on the inside, soft and elegant on the outside—and Dorian couldn't wait to make her unravel. To expose every last one of her secrets—mind, body, and soul. "Forgive me if I don't quite buy it."

"What... what are you doing?" she whispered, heart fluttering like a hummingbird, the swell of her breasts rising and falling with every frightened breath.

But the scent of her desire didn't lie.

Dorian reached up and cupped her face, dragging his thumb across those plump lips, already imagining what they'd feel like wrapped around his cock. What she'd look like on her knees, wrists bound behind her back, *begging* him for it.

But when it came to pleasure, he was a master of... Well, some might call it patience. He preferred a more accurate descriptor.

Restraint.

It was an exquisite torture, the administration of which brought him as much pleasure as the ultimate surrender.

As badly as he wanted to fuck her hot mouth, to unleash every bit of pent-up yearning her presence had stirred to life inside him, he was even more desperate to taste her. To drive her to the knife's edge between pleasure and pain, and watch her fall over the precipice, her body submitting to his every command.

He lowered his hand again, fingers skimming the top edge of her dress, the heat of her skin weakening his resolve.

A soft moan escaped her lips, despite her best efforts to contain it. Her eyelids fluttered closed.

"Ah, there's nothing quite like a bad girl in a beautiful dress," he murmured, and she arched her back, bringing her breast to his palm. Beneath his touch, her taut nipple rose against the fabric. "I suppose you think that's enough to make me fall at your feet, lapping up your lies like a starved kitten at the milk bowl."

"I didn't... I was trying to... I'm..." She tripped over her words, her breathing turning more erratic with every gentle stroke. "It's not a lie. I—"

"Shh." Dorian ran his hand down to her rib cage, thumb teasing her nipple, his other hand sliding into the hair gathered at the base of her neck. The silky knot came loose from its binds, long auburn locks tumbling over her shoulders and unleashing more of the citrus-and-vanilla scent that made his head spin.

"If I were a decent man," he said, "I'd haul you out to security and pat myself on the back for saving the poor bastard who owns this place from whatever schemes you're undoubtedly planning."

Dorian released her neck, and she opened her eyes, irises nearly swallowed by the dark pupils.

He pressed a finger to her lips to silence another excuse. The soft heat of her breath ghosted across his fingertip, the promise of her wet mouth making his cock throb.

"But since I'm *not* a decent man," he said, "I'm going to make you an offer instead. Two choices. Think very, very carefully about your response—I'm only going to ask once. Understand?"

She nodded, blood pulsing visibly beneath the pale skin of her throat, every heartbeat a seductive whisper, a promise, a warning.

Don't do this, Redthorne. You know what happens...

Ignoring the voice of reason, he gazed into her beautiful, devious eyes, his cock so hard it fucking *ached*.

"Option one," he said. "You walk out that door right now, take the elevator to the ground floor, and disappear. Don't return to this building. Don't return to this neighborhood. Forget we ever crossed paths."

"What's... what's option two?"

"Option two." Dorian lowered his mouth to hers, so close he could taste the gin on her tongue, and fisted her dress, hiking it up to reveal her bare, toned thighs. He slid a hand between them, wet heat radiating through the thin black lace of her panties. With the softest brush of his lips against hers, he whispered, "I'm tearing off this *pathetic* scrap of lace, dropping to my knees, and fucking you with my mouth until I'm absolutely *convinced* you'll never look at another painting again without recalling the time a stranger cornered you in the study at the Salvatore penthouse and forced you to come for him, again... and again... and again."

She drew a sharp breath, and he increased the pressure between her thighs, dragging his knuckles back and forth.

"So what's it going to be, little prowler? Will you go, or will you..." He arched his hand up, pushing hard against the damp fabric. "...come?"

"*Fuck*." The whisper fell against his lips, her hips rocking as Dorian restarted the slow, teasing strokes.

"What's that, gorgeous? I didn't quite catch your answer."

"Fuck off," she said, feisty until the very end. Then, with new heat blazing in her eyes, "God, I want option two. Fucking give me option two."

"Good answer, love. Because here's *my* secret." He hooked his fingers into the panties, and with a swift jerk of his wrist, tore them from her body like tissue paper. "You never really had a choice."

❆

Ready for more of vampire king Dorian and the cunning little thief out to steal more than just his heart? Grab your copy of **DARK DECEPTION** and dive into the seductive world of the Vampire Royals of New York now! Or, read on for a peek into Gabriel's world...

Looking for some Reverse Harem romance instead?

THE WITCH'S REBELS is a supernatural reverse harem series featuring five smoldering-hot guys and the kickass witch they'd kill to protect. Dark magic, steamy romance, and plenty of supernatural thrills make this series a fan-favorite!

THE WITCH'S MONSTERS is a paranormal and dark fantasy romance featuring a tough, sassy witch and the fiercely protective monsters who'll destroy anyone who touches her. Expect sizzling enemies-to-lovers romance, damaged guys who hate everyone but their witch, a high-stakes supernatural heist, and plenty of dark, twisty fun!

Sarah Piper is a witchy, Tarot-card-slinging paranormal romance and urban fantasy author. Through her signature brew of dark magic, heart-pounding suspense, and steamy romance, Sarah promises a sexy, supernatural escape into a world where the magic is real, the monsters are sinfully hot, and the witches always get their magically-ever-afters.

Readers have dubbed her work "super sexy," "imaginative and original," "off-the-walls good," and "delightfully wicked in the best ways," a quote Sarah hopes will appear on her tombstone.

Originally from New York, Sarah now makes her home in northern Colorado with her husband (though that changes frequently) (the location, not the husband), where she spends her days sleeping like a vampire and her nights writing books, casting spells, gazing at the moon, playing with her ever-expanding collection of Tarot cards, binge-watching Supernatural (Team Dean!), and obsessing over the best way to brew a cup of tea.

You can find her online at SarahPiperBooks.com, on

TikTok at @sarahpiperbooks, and in her Facebook readers group at Sarah Piper's Sassy Witches! If you're sassy, or if you need a little *more* sass in your life, or if you need more Dean Winchester gifs in your life (who doesn't?), come hang out!